1852. With the busines  finally laid to rest, Mr .... and his wife Rachel are now happily married, living in London, and blessed with a healthy baby daughter named Julia. Mr Blake has taken his late father's seat in Parliament, and his party's fortunes are on the rise—in fact they are about to overthrow the coalition government of the day.

But then the inexplicable occurs. Miss Rachel and her elderly aunt are attacked in the street by a gang of feral children, whose only purpose, it seems, is to plant a photographic portrait of a young, rich Indian lad in the old lady's handbag.

Enter the Blakes' lawyer's office boy, Octavius Guy— better known as Gooseberry—who once helped the family bring the mystery of the Moonstone to a close. Join Gooseberry, the fourteen-year-old boy detective, as he and his ragtag bunch of friends descend into London's Victorian demi-monde and underworld to ferret out the truth, while spending as much as they can of his employer's money along the way!

BOOKS BY MICHAEL GALLAGHER

Send for Octavius Guy:

Gooseberry:
Octavius Guy & The Case of the Thieving Maharajah (#1)

Octopus:
Octavius Guy & The Case of the Throttled Tragedienne (#2)

Big Bona Ogles, Boy!:
Octavius Guy & The Case of the Mendacious Medium (#3)

Oh, No, Octavius!:
Octavius Guy & The Case of the Quibbling Cleric (#4)

The Involuntary Medium:

The Bridge of Dead Things (#1)

The Scarab Heart (#2)

Gooseberry

OCTAVIUS GUY
&
The Case of the Thieving Maharajah

❧SEND FOR OCTAVIUS GUY #1❧

MICHAEL GALLAGHER

GOOSEBERRY

Send for Octavius Guy #1

Published by Seventh Rainbow Publishing, London
First published in paperback 2017
Copyright © 2014 Michael Gallagher.

The moral right of Michael Gallagher to be identified as the author of this novel has been asserted in accordance with the Copyright, Designs and Patents Act, 1988.

Cover design by Negative Negative
Cover photograph *"The Cheap Fish of St. Giles's"*
by John Thomson
Monochrome Rainbow by www.rodjonesphotography.co.uk.

ISBN 13: 978-0-9954733-3-1

Printed and bound by Amazon KDP

CONTENTS

ACKNOWLEDGEMENTS

My grateful thanks go first and foremost to Wilkie Collins, for creating that wonderful work of Victorian fiction, *The Moonstone*, in which many of the characters in this book first saw light of day. I hope I've done them justice as I make them live again. Thanks also to Lara Thomson for all her hard work, and to Malane Whillock, Alice King, and all the members of Crimes & Thrillers Reading Group at Canada Water Library for their kind support and encouragement.

The quotations used throughout are from *Robinson Crusoe* by Daniel Defoe.

A NOTE ON PALARI

Palari is a form of slang that was used by the lower classes in the nineteenth century. It most likely originates with Punch and Judy performers, and was popular with actors, costermongers, criminals, and prostitutes. Henry Mayhew documents numerous examples of its use by the 1860s in his London Labour and the London Poor. The word itself has many alternative spellings, all of which derive from the Italian word "*parlare*", meaning to talk.

A GLOSSARY OF PALARI TERMS

bona = good
eek = face [eek is a shortened form of ecaf, face spelled backwards]
dolly = pretty
feelie = child (as a noun); young (as an adjective) [from the Italian figlio, meaning son]
lallies = legs
lills = hands
nanti = no, not, none
ogles = eyes
omi = man
palone = woman
pots = teeth
riah = hair [spelled backwards]
screech = mouth
troll = stroll
varder = look at, take note of

✦

This novel is dedicated to Janet Elaine Jewel Leary, who has been like a mother to me my whole life long.
Thank you for being there. I will miss you always.

CHAPTER ONE

London. Monday, January 19th, 1852.

GEORGE AND GEORGE, THE other two office boys at Mr Bruff's law firm, sat snoring beside me on the bench, the victims of over-indulging on a plate of chops for their dinner. I gave the closer George a hefty nudge with my hip to try to claim back my fair share of the space. He came to for just a moment, blinked his eyes wearily, and then adjusted his hulking frame so that I had even less room than before.

Mr Bruff's office door swung open. Mr Bruff came out and stood there contemplating the three of us. The look on his face suggested that he didn't much care for what he saw.

'Gooseberry, with me,' he said and, closing the door behind him, made directly for the stairs. I leapt up and padded along after him.

'The local chophouse again?' he inquired, as we exited the building together into a cold and foggy Gray's Inn Square.

I nodded.

'Gooseberry, kindly inform George and George that from now on their favourite chophouse is officially off-limits.'

I don't object to Mr Bruff calling me Gooseberry, though I would have you know that it is not my real name. It's a name that's been given to me by one of Mr Bruff's clerks on account of my eyes. They bulge. At least, that's what this clerk delights in telling me almost every single day. Naturally I can't help them bulging any more than I can help being blessed with brains, and blessed with brains I am—to a far greater degree than either of the Georges, or that fool of a clerk, come to that.

I hasten to add, lest I later appear anything but entirely truthful on the subject, that having brains is not the only talent of which I am possessed, nor is Gooseberry my only nickname, which I'm sure will become clear in good time.

Mr Bruff spotted a passing cab and put his hand out to hail it. As it pulled to a halt beside us, he directed the driver to an address in Montagu Square. I recognized the address as that of his close friend and client, Mr Franklin Blake—Member of Parliament—a man to whom I have had the privilege of being useful in the past. I gripped the handrail to haul myself up to my usual seat beside the driver, but Mr Bruff clasped me by the wrist and informed me that today he required my presence in the carriage. 'There is a matter,' he said, 'that I wish to discuss.'

Despite the ominous words, Mr Bruff remained silent as the cab pulled away from the curb. It wasn't until after we'd traded High Holborn for that long stretch of road that is Oxford Street that he finally opened his mouth to speak.

'Octavius,' he said, using my proper name for a change—a name which translates from Latin as "*the eighth child*"; not that I am the eighth, you understand, I'm actually the first—'do you recall how we met?'

'I do, sir, I do,' I replied, 'although it's a good six years ago now.'

'It was a day not unlike today,' he reminisced, 'thoroughly miserable and wet. I was in Regent Street attending to a small matter of business when I observed a young lad loitering on a corner—a barefoot urchin trembling in the rain, his toes turning blue from the cold.'

Mr Bruff does like to over-sentimentalize our meeting. I imagine it helps him justify the choice he made that day. But don't be fooled by his sweeping sentimentality. This image he was painting hadn't prevented him from grabbing me by the scruff of the neck, just as I was about to remove my hand from a gentleman's pocket—with the gentleman's wallet attached. When I tactfully pointed this out to him in the cab, he immediately began to bluster:

'I had every right to march you straight in front of a magistrate, Gooseberry! Instead I chose to take pity on a young, shivering ragamuffin and offer him a position as my office boy! Can't you be grateful for that?'

I *was* grateful to him for getting me out of the Life and I told him so—before he decided to clip me round the ear. But there was more to this story than he was aware of, for I'd never got around to sharing it with him. He had always assumed I was barefoot because I was poor, but that just wasn't so. I was barefoot because one of my trusty colleagues had stolen the boots off my feet while I slept. They say there's no honour amongst thieves, and they're right. It was only because of this temporary state of boot-lessness that the old man had been able to nab me that day, for I guarantee you, at the age of eight—with my boots on—there was no swifter, slipperier pickpocket in all of London than yours truly, Octavius Guy.

It's what Mr Bruff might term "*an irony*" (a word which he assures me has everything to do with the jesting of Fate and nothing to do with scrap metal), for my lack of boots was not just my downfall. When the lawyer took pity on my poor freezing feet, it also became my salvation.

'Gooseberry, over the years you have proved yourself trustworthy, resourceful and loyal,' Mr Bruff went on, his wistful smile returning, 'and in return I have kept your former profession a secret from employees and clients alike. But today, Octavius, for the greater good, it may become necessary to divulge its nature.'

'To Mr Blake?'

Mr Bruff grunted.

'Sir, have I done something wrong?'

'No, not at all. It's quite the opposite, in fact. Mr Blake's summons was uncharacteristically vague, but the few details it gave made me think that your specialist knowledge might come in handy.'

'How so?' I asked, but Mr Bruff would say no more, preferring not to speculate until he had all the facts at his disposal. I gazed out the window. We were passing by Hyde Park and the rain was billowing about us in sheets. I tried peering into the distance to see if anything remained of the Crystal Palace, where the Great Exhibition had been held the previous year. I couldn't make out so much as a dickey-bird. Perhaps they'd already dismantled it. It set me thinking: what had they done with all those millions of panes of glass?

It was Samuel, the footman, who answered the door to us at Montagu Square. I'd met Samuel before on several occasions, just as I'd met most of Mr Blake's household. He took charge of Mr Bruff's cane and hat (though he pointedly ignored mine, obliging me to keep hold of it myself), and ushered us into the library where the family had gathered.

What a mournful sight! In the middle of the room sat a small, elderly lady, unknown to me, who was working on a piece of embroidery—or rather *not* working on it, for each time she inserted the needle, her fingers would shake and she'd burst into tears. Young Mrs Blake was on her knees at her side, her arms around her, trying in vain to comfort her as best she could.

Mrs Blake's maid, Miss Penelope, stood in the background, miserably wringing her hands in distress. It shocked me to see the complete disarray that both her locks and her clothing were in, for she was a young woman who normally took such pride in her appearance. Wisps of red hair hung loose about her face, as if she'd just been in a cat fight, and her blouse, which had been wrenched loose from her skirts, was ripped in at least three separate places.

Miss Penelope's father, the ancient Mr Betteredge—the family's faithful steward—lay slumped in a chair by the flickering fire with a tattered old book clutched to his chest. I couldn't be certain whether he was awake or asleep, for, ranked as I was as being little better than a tradesman, I was obliged to keep my distance when Mr Bruff stepped forward to greet the family.

Mr Blake, who'd been pacing listlessly about the room, grasped my employer's hand and shook it. But it was his wife—and not he—who quickly took charge of the interview.

'Mr Bruff, thank you for coming on such short notice,' she said, as she rose to her feet. 'You will remember my aunt, Mrs Merridew?'

'A pleasure as always, madam.' My employer smiled and gave a stately little bow.

The woman acknowledged it with a nod of her head. 'I had hoped to quieten my mind by occupying myself with something trivial and mundane,' she said, staring down at the embroidery in her hand, 'but it doesn't seem to be working.'

With this she broke into a fit of sobs.

'My aunt has had a rather nasty shock,' Mrs Blake explained. 'Actually, apart from my husband—who did not accompany us this morning—we *all* have.' She glanced meaningfully over her shoulder at Miss Penelope, who blinked, bit her lip, and wrung her hands again.

'My dear, as your trusted friend and your lawyer, I suggest that you start at the beginning and tell me everything that's happened.'

'Then perhaps we should sit down.'

Mr Blake drew up chairs for them both and then

resumed his pacing.

'Mr Bruff, do you consider me an imaginative woman?'

My employer gave the question some careful thought before he hazarded a reply. 'Miss Rachel, I have known you your entire life. If you ask whether I believe you possess an active imagination, then I would say, yes, you display a healthy and inquisitive one; a match for any man's. But if you ask whether I think you *imagine* things, then, no. Lawyer that I am, I would still take your word over others, were all the evidence on God's good earth to speak against you.'

Mrs Blake seemed pleased with this answer and rewarded him with a faint smile.

'Then I shall begin where I believe this mystery begins,' she said, 'even though I have no proof that it does. Last week we happened to receive an unusual number of nuisance callers. When Samuel, our footman, answered the door he would find an old beggar woman on the doorstep, with sprigs of winter heather for sale—or one of those preposterous suppliers of religious tracts—or a man who grinds knives for a living. It became ridiculous, quite ridiculous, and really rather tiresome. Occasionally he would even respond to the bell to find nobody there at all!'

'Oh, my!' exclaimed Mrs Merridew. 'How very odd! We had the same trouble at Portland Place…just before my footman gave his notice. I wondered if the bothersome callers had anything to do with his leaving, for I have no doubt they played havoc as much on his nerves as they did mine, so I asked him straight out, but he said not; rather that he was obliged to attend to his sick brother.'

'You had nuisance callers too? But, Aunt Merridew, why didn't you mention this earlier?'

'I didn't think it important, dear.'

'Surely it cannot be a coincidence! Aunt, has anything else out of the ordinary happened to you recently? For instance, have any of your windows been broken?'

'Oh, my...not that I can think of. Why do you ask?'

'Because last Friday morning Penelope discovered a broken pane of glass in the servants' quarters.'

Mr Bruff sat forward with a look of concern. 'You experienced a burglary?'

Mrs Blake shook her head. 'Apparently not, Mr Bruff, for when I had Betteredge check the inventory nothing appeared to be missing.'

'An accident, then?'

'Perhaps.' She sounded doubtful. 'Though if so, I'm surprised that no one has come forward to own up to it. It was never in my mother's nature to dock the servants' wages for breakages, nor is it in mine.'

'How very curious.'

'Curious indeed. Which brings us to the events of today. I had plans to attend an early luncheon with my aunt at her house in Portland Place and I decided to take Julia, my baby daughter, along with me. I asked Penelope to accompany us, to look after her on the way there. Then Betteredge insisted on coming, with umbrellas for us all in case it rained.'

On hearing his name, the old servant sat bolt upright in his chair.

'And rain it might have, madam,' he spluttered,

'and rain it finally did. But, in truth, that is *not* the reason I requested to come.'

'No?'

'No!' With trembling hands he held out the book he'd been clutching. His forehead was fevered with sweat. 'Just this morning I opened my copy of *Robinson Crusoe*—the one your dear late mother presented me with on the occasion of what was to be her final birthday—and what should I find there?'

He riffled through its dog-eared pages, located the passage he was looking for, and in a loud, solemn voice began to read: '"*It was the howling and yelling of those hellish creatures; and, on a sudden, we perceived two or three troops of wolves on our left, one behind us, and one on our front, so that we seemed to be surrounded with them!*"'

'You see? You see?' he cried. 'As I live by bread, madam, I knew in my heart that these self-same perils I had been directed to in this book were fated to befall you today! It was my sworn duty to come with you; no more, no less. My duty!'

An uncomfortable silence descended on the company, during which even Mr Blake stopped his pacing.

'*Robinson Crusoe*? What has *Robinson Crusoe* to do with this?' my employer demanded.

A shorter silence ensued, broken this time by Mr Blake. 'The good Betteredge firmly places his trust in Defoe to steer him safely through life,' he explained.

'I do, sir, I do!' Mr Betteredge came back, and with such passion in his voice that I wondered whether he had been drinking. 'And you would be wise to, too, Mr Bruff, lawyer though you may be!'

Lawyer that he is, my employer is not easily lost for

words, but in this case he was rendered speechless. He finally responded with a shake of his head and turned his attention back to Mrs Blake.

'Mrs Blake, will you please continue?'

She nodded and took a deep breath. 'It was a perfectly pleasant meal, Mr Bruff, but then I noticed that the weather was taking a turn for the worse. I rose to leave. My aunt had pledged to come with us, as she wished to consult my husband over the hiring of a replacement footman. I suggested that she, Julia, and I take a cab home, but Aunt Merridew refused to hear of it, saying she would prefer to walk while the rain held off. We strolled back along Wigmore Street and were just passing Portman Square when my aunt spied a woman selling flowers at the side of the road.

'"Let me stop and buy a nosegay," she begged, and opened up her handbag to retrieve her purse. Suddenly a shriek rent the air, and then another and another, as we found ourselves surrounded by a pack of howling children, lunging and pecking at us from every side.

'I don't know what would have become of us were it not for Penelope's quick thinking. She pushed me and Aunt Merridew back against the railings, thrust the baby into my arms, snatched one of her father's umbrellas and began to beat those monsters off, even as she shielded us with her body. It was so frightening! Their hands went darting everywhere—everywhere, all over us—though it was Penelope who bore the brunt of their attack. Their wailing, animal screeches finally brought people running, but the children saw them coming and swiftly scattered. By the time our rescuers got there, not one of them remained.

'We were all understandably shaken, though no one was actually hurt except Penelope here. The men who had come to our aid kindly saw us home. I had Cook clean and bathe Penelope's wounds, and asked Betteredge to make us all a restorative drink.'

Everyone looked towards the fireplace. Exhausted by his earlier outburst, the steward had fallen fast asleep.

'It was only while we were recovering,' Mrs Blake continued, 'that I realized the attack might have been purposely staged, perhaps to try to rob us, so we all checked our capes and belongings to see if anything had been taken.'

'And?'

'Well, this is the most perplexing part of all, Mr Bruff. *Nothing* had been taken.'

The lawyer's eyes narrowed. 'But Mr Blake's summons...I was led to believe—'

'I repeat, nothing had been taken. *But something had most definitely been left.*'

CHAPTER TWO

'LEFT?'

'Inserted into Aunt Merridew's bag. Here, see for yourself.'

Mrs Blake rose and walked over to the table. She retrieved a small palm-sized leather case, not unlike a notebook, and carried it back to my employer.

'Open it.'

Mr Bruff turned the case over in his hands, found the tiny clasp at the side, and unlatched it. All I could see was the occasional glint from where I was standing, but even so I was ninety-nine percent certain that what he was holding was a daguerreotype: a photograph on a sheet of silvered copper, mounted behind glass in a plush-lined case. There was a time not so long ago when I would have hopped up on a chair to get a better look. I should like to be able to tell you that I have since learned the value of patience, but it wouldn't be true. What I have learned is that the upper classes don't appreciate your boots on their furniture, no matter how pressing your needs may be.

'So,' my employer summed up, having studied the photograph at some length, 'both you and your aunt were subjected to nuisance callers; a pane of glass was found broken in the servants' quarters; and then today a gang of hooligans attacked you in broad daylight— not to rob you of anything, but to place this about your aunt's person?'

'It sounds incredible, Mr Bruff, I grant you, but how else can that daguerreotype have found its way into my aunt's handbag?'

'Mrs Merridew, do you recognize either of the people in this photograph?'

'No, Mr Bruff, they're perfect strangers.'

'Mrs Blake?'

'I'm sorry, I don't.'

'Mr Blake?'

'I've never seen either of them in my life. But observe, sir—the boy. The tone of his skin…his manner of dress. Though the man's a Caucasian—and most probably English, judging by the cut of his suit— the boy is an Indian, is he not?'

Mr Bruff nodded. 'And an extremely wealthy one, by the look of it.' He peered at the daguerreotype again. 'It's a very formal portrait,' he remarked, 'carefully composed and beautifully rendered. It's not the work of an amateur. And yet, notice the boy's scarred right eye; there's been no attempt to disguise the lad's disfigurement.'

'You don't suppose that this could have anything to do with that accursed Moonstone diamond, do you? I had hoped I'd put that business behind me for good.'

'Because the lad's Indian? No, Mr Blake, your investigations were faultless. I'm sure the boy's race is purely a coincidence.'

'Then perhaps someone's trying to discredit me. The political party I serve may be in opposition at the moment but, trust me, sir, things are about to change. This unholy coalition—which would take its grain from other countries instead of from our own worthy farmers—they're on their way out and they know it! I wouldn't put it past them to pull some dastardly stunt to embarrass us first.'

'If they were trying to embarrass you, Franklin, why give the photograph to my aunt?' Mrs Blake inquired of her husband. 'Why not to you?'

'A very good question,' said Mr Bruff. 'But what I'd like to know is why a street gang would go to these extraordinary lengths to do such a thing? That is the crux of this matter. What we need is someone versed in their ways who might help us unravel this puzzle. Gooseberry, I think the time has come for you to tell us what you can.'

I stepped forward, expecting to be quizzed about my credentials. Instead I found myself being fussed over handsomely by Mr Blake.

'Upon my word! Gooseberry!' he cried, shaking my hand and slapping me on the back. 'I didn't see you there!'

Mr Bruff quickly intervened and directed me to business. 'What is your opinion,' he asked, 'of all that you've heard here today?'

'First, can I please see the daguerreotype?'

'"*May* I see the daguerreotype"',' Mr Bruff corrected

me, as he handed over the picture.

If anything it was even grander than I had imagined: a portrait of a man and a boy seated side by side in chairs that could almost pass for thrones, in what can only be described as an opulently—and quite exotically—furnished room.

'Gooseberry, your contribution, please.'

I passed the picture back and turned to address Mrs Blake. 'Gangs such as you describe, miss, work in two particular ways, both of which depend on creating as much chaos and confusion as possible.'

'Why?' she asked.

'Well, to dazzle people's senses, miss. It makes them slow to react.'

'I see. Go on.'

'In the first, the gang runs in, causes a commotion, grabs what it is they're after, then scatters as soon as they can. It requires a little planning, but hardly any skill, which is why the second way is infinitely more satisfying—'

'Satisfying?'

As I considered what my response should be to this, I placed my hat, which their footman Samuel had obliged me to keep hold of, down on the nearest chair, earning myself a look of reproach from Mrs Blake's maid, Miss Penelope.

'Well, intellectually satisfying, if you like, miss. While the gang is wreaking chaos and everyone's attention is diverted, somebody else—someone on the spot who seems quite unconnected with any of the troublemakers—he stealthily slips the desired items inside his jacket—an overly-large jacket like the one

I'm wearing now.' *Or down his trousers. Or under his hat.* 'Once the gang has scarpered, that person calmly walks away, taking his booty with him.' *While lifting wallet after wallet as he saunters through the crowd. Ah, my glory days, indeed!* 'Later the gang meets up at some predetermined location to share out their spoils—in accordance with each person's rank, of course, and the amount of risk each person took.' *Well, the spoils that they know about, that is.*

Mrs Blake looked at me thoughtfully and asked, 'Gooseberry, how do you know all of this?'

The time had come to own up to my past. I'd been thinking about how best to present it, and it seemed to me that what was called for here was a judicious mixture of remorse, honesty, and diffidence.

'Though it shames me to say it,' *remorse*, 'there was no swifter, slipperier pickpocket in all of London,' *honesty*, 'than…well, me, miss—your humble servant—Octavius Guy.' *Diffidence dispensed in a generous measure.*

Mrs Blake burst out laughing.

'Please, Mrs Blake, it's true.'

'Gooseberry, you really mustn't joke.'

'I'm not joking, miss.'

'I don't believe it for a moment!'

Mr Bruff gave a cautious lawyer's cough that managed to get everyone's attention. 'He's telling the truth,' he said quietly, and shot Mrs Blake a meaning-ful look.

'But this is Gooseberry we're talking about! Our Gooseberry! He's no thief!'

'If he's telling us the truth, then I think he should be made to prove it,' said Mr Blake, a mischievous grin breaking out on his face that even his thick, black beard couldn't hide. 'I propose a challenge. Gooseberry, come and try to pick my pocket!'

'Please, sir—I don't want to pick your pocket.'

'But I insist,' he said, stepping closer and closer till there was barely a foot between us. With everyone watching (save for the good Mr Bruff, whose features plainly registered his disapproval), Mr Blake leaned forward so that our noses were practically touching. On reflex, I found myself stumbling backwards, a move that Mr Blake took as a sign of defeat.

'So much for the swiftest, slipperiest pickpocket in all of London,' he laughed and, like a performer taking his curtain call, turned and bowed deeply to his wife.

'Franklin, look,' she advised him, pointing her finger at me.

Mr Blake looked. His mouth dropped open. He stared, blinking in amazement, at the silver cigarette case in my hand.

He patted the vicinity of his jacket's left inside-breast pocket, feeling for something that was no longer there. Out of the corner of my eye I saw Mrs Blake's aunt place her embroidery in her handbag and hug the handbag to her chest. My heart suddenly crumpled; I should have realized how people might not take too kindly to discovering a thief in their midst.

Mr Blake regarded me solemnly for several long seconds. 'How did you manage it?' he asked at last. 'I didn't feel a thing. Not a thing.'

'It's just a skill I have,' I replied, preparing to duck his blows as I handed him back his case.

'During my travels in the East, five men attempted

to pick my pocket—and five men ended up regretting it. But you! That wasn't skill, young man; it was art! By all that's wondrous, you're going to have to teach me how you did that!'

'Teach you to steal things? No, Mr Blake! It wouldn't be right.'

Mrs Blake arched her eyebrow at the both of us and said, 'I'm glad to see that one of you is old enough and wise enough to appreciate right from wrong. So, tell me, Gooseberry, expert pickpocket and moral compass that you are, in your opinion, what do you think happened to us today?'

'It's very hard to say, miss. I can't begin to fathom why a gang would want to plant something on you, especially if it's something that holds no apparent meaning for any of you. However, from what you've told me, I'm fairly sure that the method they employed was the second one I outlined. Your attackers were simply the distraction. Somebody else—someone on the spot, seemingly unconnected—was responsible for slipping that photograph into your aunt's handbag.'

'But who?' she asked. 'The only people present were my aunt, myself, Penelope and her father, and my baby daughter Julia. You surely don't suggest that one of us did it?'

'I beg your pardon, miss, but you're mistaken.'

'Gooseberry, I know who was there. There was nobody else, believe me.'

'But there was, miss. There was the flower girl; the one selling flowers by the side of the road. Did anyone see where she went to?'

Mrs Blake stared. 'She was with us, I think. I really

can't remember. Aunt Merridew, do you recall?'

'I was too terrified to notice, dear. I expect my nerves will be shattered for weeks.'

'Penelope, what about you?'

'I'm sorry, Miss Rachel,' the maid responded shakily, speaking for the first time since we'd entered the room. 'I was too busy battling off those horrid beasts of children. I have no idea where the woman went.'

Mrs Blake glanced across the room to where her faithful retainer lay dozing. Choosing not to wake the old man, she turned her attention back to me.

'So you think it was the woman selling flowers?'

'I certainly think it's possible, miss. I can't see who else it might be. Do you think you can describe her?'

Mrs Blake frowned. 'She was a big girl. I remember that.'

'Very big. And certainly no beauty,' added her aunt. 'A poor, ungainly thing, crouching on her haunches beside her basket. I recall seeing her pock-marked face and taking pity on her, which is why I insisted that we stop to buy a posy.'

'I don't remember pock-marks,' Miss Penelope cut in, apologizing for the interruption, 'but I have to say she wasn't all that big.' On finding herself the centre of attention, she quickly looked away. A moment later she was wringing her hands again.

'Of course, I could be wrong,' Mrs Merridew admitted, 'but I honestly don't think that I am. You see, although I couldn't say why exactly, I was truly fascinated by the creature. There was something utterly compelling about her that I couldn't quite put my finger on.'

Miss Penelope's objection aside, a picture was already beginning to form in my mind. 'What colour was her hair?' I asked. 'And how was she dressed?'

'Coarse, dark brown shoulder-length hair, parted in the middle and pulled back into a bun,' the aunt reeled the description off excitedly, her distrust of me temporarily forgotten. 'Yellow cap and ribbons instead of the usual headscarf affair. A light-grey blouse, which hung from her shoulders like a sack, and a tattered, dark-grey skirt. A filthy red shawl, one end of which she held across her mouth, I imagine to try to hide her scars.'

'I remember the shawl,' Mrs Blake agreed, her nose wrinkling up at the thought. 'I wouldn't put it anywhere near my lips.'

'Broad-shouldered? Arms like hams?'

'Why, yes, Gooseberry; that's right.'

'And softly spoken?'

'So softly spoken I could hardly make out anything she said,' Mrs Blake replied. 'Aunt Merridew had to ask the price of the posy several times.'

The old lady nodded in agreement.

'She kept her eyes averted? Never once looked at you directly?'

'Gooseberry? Do you *know* her?'

I was almost positive that I did, back in the Life. Everyone knew her—Big Bertha, they called her. Bertha, whose real name was Bert.

I can't rightly say whether it was out of a sense of propriety or a sense of embarrassment that I chose to keep the delicate nature of Bertha's gender to myself. Not that it mattered either way; the important thing was that we now had a lead.

Mr Bruff wound up the meeting by promising the Blakes that I would follow up on it the very next day. He also requested they entrust him with the daguerreotype, as he had an idea of his own he wished to pursue.

'May I please take another look at it,' I asked on the cab journey back, remembering just in time his strictures over the use of the verbs *can* and *may*. He pulled it out and handed it to me, but I was sorely disappointed. I had hoped to divine some link between the people in the photograph and Big Bertha. But study it as I might, nothing came to mind.

The streets were deserted and bracingly chilly as I made my way homeward up the Gray's Inn Road, stopping only to collect a couple of eel pies and some macaroons from the eating house on the way. Turning east, I set off along the New Road, past the site of the old smallpox hospital. They're in the process of building a railway terminus there, which locals claim will bring train-loads of people from Scotland—though why any of them would want to visit my own little part of the world was a complete mystery to me. But, ah, the wonders of living in the Golden Age of Steam, eh? Board a train in the morning in Edinburgh and disembark in the evening at King's Cross!

I have lodgings off the Caledonian Road, or the "*Cally Road*" as it's commonly called. There's talk of them erecting a cattle market up by the prison, but till then the Cally remains the principal route into Smithfield for every drover herding his cattle down from the north. The area's much quieter at night, mind, without a single cow's lowing to be heard; so quiet in fact that, with your window open, you can hear the lapping of the nearby canal and the gentle thud of the coal barges moored up together in pairs.

That night, as I rounded the corner, I saw that my window was closed, but a flicker of light in the glass warned me someone was already home. I ran up the stairs two at a time and silently pushed open the door.

'Octavius!' came the shout of pure joy from inside.

A small, lithe figure of a boy cannonballed into me from halfway across the room, gripping me so tightly that I nearly let go of the pies. My younger brother Julius.

'Did you have a good day today, Octavius? Did you get to do anything interesting? We sold all the fish on the stall by four o'clock, so I got to come home early. I came straight here, Octavius, just like you said to do; I didn't hang round. Did you bring us anything for supper? It doesn't matter if you didn't because I had a hot potato for my dinner.'

I wriggled out of his grasp and, like a conjurer, made a show of presenting him with the pies. His eyes lit up like beacons.

'Eel pies?' he cried, dancing with excitement. 'You know they're my favourite!'

We set the table and ate, both of us savouring for as long as we could the rich jellied meat in its crust. Afterwards I scoured the plates with cold ashes from the stove while Julius collected his supply of scrap paper—scavenged from the waste bins at the office—and then proudly retrieved his treasured pencil from the shelf.

'What word will we do tonight?' he asked.

CHAPTER TWO

'I don't know...what word do you think will be useful?' This was a routine we repeated every night.

'How about "*sprats*"?' he suggested, after a moment's thought. 'We had sprats on the stall today.'

I carefully wrote down the word for him and he began to copy it. I sat and watched him as he wrote, his face set hard with concentration and his small, pink tongue sticking out. I could have spent a lifetime watching him that way, but eventually the candle burned too low.

We were up the next day before dawn, for we both had early starts; Julius off to his fish stall in Old Street and me on my hunt to find Bertha. Bertha was a creature of habit, so I knew where he'd probably be, the day in question being a Tuesday. The flower market at Covent Garden.

The sun was still struggling to rise as I made my way down Drury Lane and into Long Acre, dodging wagons loaded to the brim with fresh produce. Although it was early, the piazza was crowded and the streets leading into it jammed. I passed stalls stacked high with cauliflowers and cabbages, swerving to avoid the bustling porters. Did my fingers itch to perform as they once had? No. But I did wonder if Mr Bruff had given any thought to what he was asking of me, requiring me, as it did, to rub shoulders again with my former partners from the Life.

If I remembered correctly, Bertha's pitch was on the west side of the square, at the rear of the Actors' Church. Six years may have passed since I'd last seen him, but if I knew Bertha, he'd rather kill than give up such a desirable site.

And I was right. As I turned the corner, there he was. Dressed in grey and draped in his dirty red cape, his head bowed low to show off the bright yellow cap and ribbons he wore, he was squatting on the pavement and looking quite ungainly as he sorted through his basket full of flowers.

He must have seen my boots as I approached, for all at once he pulled his shawl across his mouth, bowed his head a little lower, and quietly began to mumble in a deep, hoarse whisper: 'Buy a nice posy from a poor, honest woman, sir? Or a bouquet for your sweet, faithful wife?'

'Hello, Bertha.'

Big Bertha's face shot up. 'Oh, my Gawd, as I live and breathe!' he squawked. 'I'd recognize those bulging big ogles anywhere! It's you. It's young Octopus, back from the dead or Van Diemen's Land!'

Octopus. My other nickname.

CHAPTER THREE

I LIKE TO THINK that I am a man of the world—
or, to be more accurate, having attained the grand age
of fourteen, I like to think I am now *two-thirds* of a
man of the world—and I would have you know that
in my time I have seen both men dressed as women
and women dressed as men. Of these, some have been
most convincing. Many, less so. Bertha, I'm afraid,
didn't even make it into this category. There was
nothing feminine or effeminate about him whatsoever.
In a sense he was simply a big, jowly bloke in a dress.
No wonder Mrs Blake's aunt had been fascinated by
him. I'm sure she'd never seen anything like him in
her life.

'Look at you!' he cried, rubbing his eyes as if he'd
seen a ghost. 'My, ain't you grown! Why, you're almost
a fully-fledged omi,' he said, meaning "*man*" in *Palari*,
the actors' slang he was apt to use. 'So where the hell
you been, then?'

'Well, I wasn't sent to some Australian penal
colony, if that's what you imagined.'

He blinked. 'Wot, then?'

'I simply needed a break from the Life, that's all.'

'But where d'you take yourself off to? Ain't no one just disappears like that.'

No? I'd managed it pretty well up until now.

'I went to live in Edinburgh,' I lied.

'Edinbra?' He considered this carefully. 'Ain't that somewhere up norf?'

By the time I agreed that it was, he'd already begun to lose interest. Instead he was employing his critical eye to give me a quick once-over.

'Well, well, well! You've grown to be quite a looker, ain't ya? You seeing anyone, then? If not, I'd be more than happy to—'

'No, Bertha, I'm really flattered, truly I am, but…'

'No, no, no! I ain't talking 'bout *me*!' He wagged a fleshy finger in my face. 'You got to learn to lower those sights of yours, lad. No, I was trying to tell you 'bout this matrimonial bureau wot I runs now—strictly just a sideline, o' course. A young omi such as yourself, I could get you fixed up in a jiffy.'

'But what if I don't want to be fixed up?'

He wasn't listening. Something or someone had caught his attention on the other side of the piazza.

''Ere, Florrie, get those scrawny, little hips over 'ere now! Octopus, I want you to meet Florrie. Florrie, this here's Octopus.'

'Octopus?' The girl Bertha had summoned was gawking shamelessly at my eyes. 'That's an unusual name,' she said. She was dressed, as most of the market girls were, in a blouse and skirt, with a shawl draped over her shoulders. Her blonde hair was pulled back from her face and tied up with a black velvet band.

'Forget those bona big ogles, girl,' chortled Bertha, referring to my eyes. 'It's his lills you ought to be worried about. 'E's got eight of 'em.'

'Eight?' Florrie's gaze dropped to my hands in a panic. She gave a sigh of relief when she saw that I only had two.

'This young omi used to troll through the streets lifting wallets left, right, and centre—just like an octopus would if it 'ad any real appreciation of money! You keep your eye on him, girl, or his lills will be all over you in no time.' The girl blushed as Bertha gave a deep throaty chuckle. 'First assignation's free,' he continued, now addressing me, 'it's the second that'll cost ya; strictly no third unless it's a wedding!' Bertha gave me a big, theatrical wink. 'Got to make it look proper, see; I won't have no one saying I'm procuring. Me, I'm a respectable woman!'

Florrie and I regarded each other in a state of nervous embarrassment. She looked almost alarmed; I'm sure I did too.

'Young people these days!' griped Bertha. 'No sense of romance! Go on, Florrie, if he ain't going to kiss ya and paw yeh, you may as well give us a hand with these posies.'

The two of them knelt on the pavement and began binding stems together with green twine.

'So how's the flower business going?' I asked. 'Everything in the garden blooming?'

'Mustn't grumble, mustn't grumble,' Bertha grumbled. ''Ere, wot do you think of my new line of patter?' He bowed his head, pulled his shawl across his mouth, and started whispering the same catchphrase he'd whispered before: 'Buy a nice posy from a poor, honest woman, sir? Or a bouquet for your sweet, faithful wife?'

'It's good. Really good.' It was a definite improvement on the one I remembered: "*Varder me dolly flowers, sir.*"—meaning, look at my pretty flowers—"*Get 'em quick before they die.*"

Bertha grinned.

'I hear you were over on Wigmore Street yesterday,' I said.

The grin faded. 'Oh? And where d'yeh hear that?'

'Some friends of mine were accosted…by a gang. The odd thing is, when I asked them about it, they managed to describe you perfectly.'

'Friends of yours, eh?'

'People I care about, yes.'

He took a moment to digest this. 'Shame,' he said. 'Seems like a poor, decent woman can't go nowhere no more wiffout being set on by ruffians.'

'Wigmore Street's a bit outside your territory, Bertha. And that got me thinking. This job had to be special—planned to order by someone much higher up.'

'Well, I wouldn't know, 'cos I wasn't there!' he bawled.

We eyed each other warily, like a pair of fractious circus tigers, until Bertha finally cracked and looked away. It wasn't stalemate yet, however, for I still had one move left up my sleeve.

'So you weren't the one who slipped the daguerre-otype in the old lady's bag?' I said.

For the second time in twenty minutes, Bertha's pock-marked face shot up. Florrie, who'd been watching our little exchange with increasing discomfort, rose to her feet and announced she was leaving.

'No, you stay right where you are,' Bertha growled at her, even though he was glaring at me. 'It's young Octopus here wot needs to leave. Go on, Octopus—' And here he bellowed a two-word Anglo-Saxon phrase at me, causing everyone in the square to look.

I beat a tactical retreat into the bustling piazza and hid myself behind a barrow-load of celery. I'd purposely kicked the hornets' nest and I wanted to see what Bertha would do next. I didn't have to wait long. Leaving his stall in Florrie's care, he threw his shawl over his shoulders and set off at a cracking pace down King Street. Despite the considerable number of pedestrians, he made an easy target to follow. His yellow cap and ribbons bobbed a good six inches above most of the heads in the crowd.

At the corner he turned north, as if heading towards Long Acre, but then pulled up short outside a public house. I knew the pub from years ago, but its reputation had since grown: they regularly staged bare-knuckled prize fights there now. It was the Lamb and Flag, referred to hereabouts as the Bucket of Blood. After a moment's hesitation, Bertha went inside.

I crept up to the windows and peered in. Though the hour was still early, business was brisk, as it tends to be for any pub on a market day. I scoured the room, but there was no sign of Bertha. I stepped back a little and gazed up at the windows above. Was one of the old crew up there, holding court in a private suite? Perhaps even Ned himself, if he still happened to be in charge. How would he react when he heard I was back, I wondered?

It seemed as if I had a choice. Burst in and confront him, or whoever it was who was running things now—a strategy that hadn't played out so well with Bertha—or wait and see what would happen. I took a coin from my pocket and flipped it. Tails. Better to wait.

I returned to the corner and stood by the railings, watching and biding my time. Ten minutes passed, and then twenty. At last the door opened and Bertha emerged.

I held my ground for a moment as he marched away, curious to see if anyone else would appear. When no one did, I sped off after him, just in time to see him cross the road into Bedford Street. At the Strand he turned left and began to head east, past Temple Bar into Fleet Street. The pavement here was not so crowded, so I could afford to fall back a little.

Still he trundled eastwards, past St Paul's, past London Bridge, and past the Tower. Now came the docks with their innumerable ships moored up in miniature cities. Gulls reeled and circled among the masts against the steel-grey, mid-morning sky. Surrounded by beer-bellied dockers, Bertha was in his element, lapping up the hoots and wolf whistles he'd started to attract.

Somewhere between the London Dock and the East London Dock, Bertha paused. He peered to his right, then took a road that led down towards the river. A few minutes later he made another quick turn, this time to his left. As I came round the corner, I saw that he'd reached his destination. He'd joined a small line of people queuing up outside an octagonal marble tower. As those in the queue were all dressed rather fashionably, Bertha stuck out like the proverbial sore thumb. So did the tower, come to that. Being new and being built of pale-grey marble, it seemed truly at odds with the neighbouring warehouses, all of which had seen better days. Gradually the line grew shorter and Bertha vanished within.

I followed a minute or two later, in time to see him picking a fight with the man in the ticket booth. 'But it's only a penny!' I heard the chap saying, as I popped my head round the entrance.

'A penny's a penny!' growled Bertha. 'And I'm not some damned sightseer; I'm 'ere on business! Now bleedin' well let me in!'

Grudgingly the fellow complied, operating the narrow brass turnstile to allow him to pass.

I made my way across the blue and white tiled floor and handed over my penny. The chap still looked livid from his encounter with Bertha, so I was dreading asking for a receipt—a matter of some necessity for me, for Mr Bruff's clerk who handles the petty cash claims is a tyrant where receipts are concerned. But before I'd plucked up the courage to do so, he pressed some kind of lever, and I was forcibly propelled through the turnstile gates and spat out the other side. I suppose I *could* have knocked on the back door of the ticket booth, but even I have my pride. In front of me loomed a doorway. Without knowing quite what to expect, I squared my shoulders and stepped on through.

I found myself at the top a circular shaft, lit entirely by gaslight. A lengthy spiral staircase descended forty feet or so to a marble floor below. Here and there, there were landings to break the descent, hung with paintings of palaces and waterfalls. There was even the odd plaster statue or two. Ghostly organ music echoed up from the depths, *The Marseillaise*, by the sound of it. Below me, Bertha had nearly reached the bottom of the stairs. I quickened my pace; I didn't want to lose him in the crowd.

He barely glanced at the sideshow attractions dotted about the room (*"Your Fortune Told"*, *"The Egyptian Rune Reader"*, *"The Monkey Answers All Your Questions"*) and made directly for the pair of tunnel entrances that stood opposite the stairs. Choosing the right-hand one, he set off along it, with me still in hot pursuit.

The tunnel seemed to stretch for as far as the eye could see. Strategically-positioned gas lamps lit the way and every so often there was a gap in the wall that allowed access from one tunnel to the other. Stalls selling various lines of cheap goods were set up in these gaps, staffed in the main by pallid young women, with skin that was even paler than mine. Ahead of me, Bertha drew up in front of one such stall and began to examine the merchandise. As I huddled against the tunnel wall, I felt a drop of ice-cold water hit the back of my neck and trickle its way down my collar. By now I had a very good idea where I was.

Bertha was on the move again. As I passed the stall where he'd stopped, I glanced down at the ribbons he'd been inspecting. Each had the words "*Souvenir of the Thames Tunnel*" woven through it, confirming my suspicion. Here I was in the world's first sub-aquatic tunnel, well below the bed of the Thames, with ten thousand tons of water pressing down on me!

My moment of reflection came at a cost. When I looked up, Bertha had vanished.

He couldn't have gone far, I reasoned; my attention had wavered for a few seconds at most. I kept going in the direction he'd been heading. To my left was another gap, this time with a stall selling magic lantern slides. Twenty yards on, there was another, this one a coffee shop decked out with tables, nearly all of which were occupied. An eccentric-looking waiter in a coster-monger's jacket, stitched with rows of mother-of-pearl buttons, weaved his way between the tables delivering drinks and light refreshments. Bertha couldn't have got any further than this.

I moved swiftly through the underwater coffee shop, searching the customers' faces, till I came out in the adjacent tunnel. I peered up and down. Bertha was nowhere to be seen. I retraced my steps back to the shaft, checking each of the stalls as I went. As impossible as it seemed, Bertha had given me the slip.

I loitered at the foot of the stairs and watched the procession of people. I made a tour of the room and examined the organ that was currently churning out *Rule Britannia*. Driven by steam, it somehow managed to play itself. I considered consulting the monkey, the one that "*Answers All Your Questions*", for I had several that were puzzling me deeply. The problem was his method. Two nuts were placed on a board before him; one on a square that said "*yes*", the other on a square that said "*no*". The nut he chose first indicated his answer. *Is Bertha still in the tunnel? Is Bertha still in the right-hand tunnel?* At a penny a shot, and with only yes-or-no answers to guide me, it could cost a small fortune to locate Bertha in this manner. I took out a coin, but it wasn't for the monkey. Should I stay or should I go? I flipped it.

Heads. Stay, then.

I wandered back to the coffee shop, took a seat, and ordered a piece of cake from the man in the button-clad jacket. Idly I wondered where he kept his supplies, for he was doing a roaring trade.

The afternoon wore on. I began to notice that nearly everything in the tunnel cost a penny. It was rather clever, really; for the price of a couple of nice, fat herrings anyone could buy a piece of tat to remind themselves of their time spent down here. I bought a candle at one stall, then moved on to the next, which just happened to sell writing equipment. It was staffed by a young woman with bright auburn hair, whose mouth gaped open in an undisguised yawn. I couldn't resist following her example and gave a big yawn myself.

'Who buys these things?' I asked, as I browsed through the pencils and dip-pens laid out on the white marble counter-top, each stamped with the brand, "*Souvenir of the Thames Tunnel*".

'Tourists,' she replied without enthusiasm.

'How much?' I asked, selecting a fine looking pencil for Julius. 'No, don't tell me. It's a penny, right?' I saw her eyes roll towards the ceiling. 'Oh, and may I have a receipt, please?' I added.

'*A receipt for a penny*?'

'If you would be so kind…?'

She threw me a look of pure hatred.

Before too long the music ground to a halt and stewards began to herd everyone out. 'Ladies and Gentlemen! The Tunnel is closing in fifteen minutes. Please make your way to the exits!'

I didn't need to be told twice. I nipped up the stairs and was outside in a shot. Night had fallen, but it couldn't have been late. I took shelter in a nearby doorway and watched as people emerged—first the patrons, who took their sweet time about it, then the staff (including the monkey), who were champing at the bit to get home. The waiter from the coffee shop had changed out of his jacket. He looked positively run-of-the-mill without it. The last person to leave was the man from the ticket booth; it was he who was in charge of locking up. He took the task seriously— he checked the doors twice before tucking his keys in his pocket. I followed him as he set off towards the river, making, as it turned out, for the nearest public house.

Retrieving the receipt for my pencil, I crumpled it a little (to add an air of authenticity), and ran up and tapped him on the elbow.

'Yes?' he said, peering down at me, as his fingers closed round the handle of the pub's glazed door.

'Sir,' I addressed him in my most earnest voice, 'I believe that you might have dropped this.' I held out the receipt for inspection.

He looked at it, recognized it for what it was, and

dismissed my claim with a wave of his hand. Then he pulled the door open and stepped into the pub, shutting me out on the footpath.

Though I kept my face blank, on the inside I was beaming, for I now had his full set of keys.

CHAPTER FOUR

GETTING IN WAS EASY. The big key opened the main door. Once I was in, I locked it behind me and lit the candle I'd bought. I thought the turnstile might prove problematic, but for some reason the mechanism had been disengaged, and now it turned freely. By simple trial and error I found the key to the shaft, unlocked the door, and made my way down the stairs.

It was extraordinary the transformation that had taken place in little under an hour. Before the Thames Tunnel had seemed like a fairground; now, minus the gaslights, the organ, and the ebb and flow of the patrons, it felt more like a crypt. The only sound to be heard was the occasional pitter-patter of the river raining down from above.

I retraced my steps down the right-hand passage, keeping my wary eyes peeled. The marble counters had been cleared of their merchandise, so it was hard to gauge the distance I'd come. Ahead of me lay the coffee shop, its tables now stripped of their linen. Though I had no idea where the rest of the tat had gone, I knew exactly where the coffee shop's provisions were stored, for I'd kept a careful eye on the waiter each time he went to fetch more cakes.

I sent up a quick prayer to St Quentin, patron saint of locksmiths, that one of my new-found keys would fit the storeroom door, for though there may be no swifter, slipperier pickpocket in all of London, I have to admit to a certain ham-fistedness when it comes to picking locks. I knew the theory, of course, but had always had a tough time putting it into practice.

I found the key on the fifth attempt and felt the bolt slide back as the teeth engaged. Cautiously I prised open the door and took a look inside.

Running parallel with the tunnel, the room was narrow and long, and smelled overwhelmingly of coffee. As I shone my candle around, I spied a large cast-iron coffee grinder in the corner. Most of the space was taken up with shelving on which dozens of cakes— mainly Dundee cakes and Bakewell tarts—were stored. Further down there were bottles; fortified wines, by the looks of it.

Suddenly I heard a moan—a low muffled keening that originated at the far end of the room. I made my way towards it and found Bertha trussed up like a chicken, with both his hands shackled to the wall. One side of his face had been beaten, so it was a bloodied, swollen eye that stared up at me in surprise.

'Octopus?' he said, once I'd fished out the filthy tea towel that was crammed into his mouth. 'Wot the hell are you doing 'ere?'

'It looks as if I'm saving your hide,' I replied, glancing over my shoulder at the array of bottles.

''Ere, where you going?' he demanded, when I left him for a moment to collect a few bits and pieces. I returned a second later with a bottle of port and a knife.

'Careful with that,' he kept squawking, as I sawed through his ropes. 'Oi! That's me bleedin' arm, that is!'

'Stop complaining! Here, take a swig of this.' I opened the bottle and held it to his lips. He drank noisily, guzzling the plummy, sweet liquid with obvious relish.

'Ooh, that feels better,' he sighed. 'Now, how's about getting me out of these?' He raised his shackled wrists to show me his handcuffs. Grimly I stared at the lock.

'Prepare yourself, Bertha. This may take me some time.'

It did, even when I'd found a nail to use as a pick. Back in the day, I really should have paid more attention to Billy the Shim when he tried to instruct me in the mysterious ways of locks. *No slower, sloppier lock-pick in all of London* hasn't quite the same ring to it as my regular sobriquet, as true as it undoubtedly is.

Between Bertha's many calls for further refreshment and my own frequent breaks to prevent my fingers cramping, I have no real idea how long it took me— but by the time I'd finally managed to spring the catch, my hands were aching, Bertha was paralytic, and the candle had burned to a stump.

'Here, Bertha, put your arm around my shoulder.'

I slipped a few choice items from the shelves into my jacket and then, supporting him as best I could, we staggered to the door. But as it swung open, I instinctively drew back.

Something was clearly wrong. The gaslights were lit and one quick glance was all it took to establish that Bertha and I were no longer alone. When I say that there were young women on the counters, this time I mean they were literally *seated* on the counters. And parading back and forth in front of them, eager to sample their wares, were seedy, drooling men of all shapes and sizes—and of all ages and manner of dress, come to that.

Bertha began to giggle. 'Looks like the night shift's begun.'

'Night shift?'

'The Fair Maids of Wapping. 'Ospitality offered to gentry and sailors alike, every night 'cepting Sundays.' The words came out in intoxicated fits and starts. 'Nice touch, that, about the Sundays—makes it look real proper. All Johnny's idea.'

'Johnny?'

'You remember Johnny!'

I shook my head.

'Nah, 'course you do, Octopus. Johnny Knight. Goes by the name Johnny Full Moon these days—Johnny Full-Moon-Every-Bleedin' Knight.'

'*Johnny Knight's running things now?*'

Bertha nodded.

Oh, I remembered Johnny, all right. We'd risen up through the ranks together—me because of my skills; Johnny because he took risks...lunatic risks—hence the reference to the full moon, I imagined. Even when I eventually came to outrank him, I was always wary of Johnny, for Johnny Knight wasn't just some mad risk-taker, he also had a nasty vicious streak. What, I wondered, had become of Ned, the man who'd been in charge when I was around?

'Bertha, listen; this is important! Will Johnny be here tonight?'

'Might be. Wot day's it?'

'It's a Tuesday.'

'Then, nah, nah, he won't. Tuesdays, Thursdays, and Saturdays, they're market days, see. He'll be at the Bucket of Blood, overseein' 'is fights.'

'But these girls…they all work for Johnny?' They'd be bound to notice a fourteen-year-old boy and a man in a dress in their midst. The question was, what would they do about it?

As if reading my thoughts, Bertha pulled his shawl across the lower half of his face and steered me rather drunkenly into the tunnel.

'Concentrate, Octopus!' he whispered in my ear. 'You're an omi and I'm a palone,' by which he meant that I was a man and he was a woman. 'Wot's more natural than a young omi like yourself desiring my company for the evenin'? We're just taking a little walk together, see, to find some place a bit more private. Who could object to that?'

His plan seemed to be working. We'd made it all the way to the shaft before anyone clocked that something was amiss. The girl I'd requested a receipt from, the one with the auburn tresses, spotted me and began raising all hell.

'What's *he* doing down here?' she shrieked, pointing in my direction. But the client she was with wasn't having it; he clearly had other things on his mind. He grabbed her wrists, forced himself on top of her, and started smothering her cries with his kisses. The more she protested the more passionate he became. As quickly as I could—which was not quickly at all—I bundled Bertha up the stairs.

I had no idea what I would find at the top, but I prayed it wouldn't be the chap whose keys I had lifted. It wasn't. It was some oily-haired toad-of-a-man, who, according to Bertha's overly-loud whisperings, ran the ticket booth in the Rotherhithe shaft.

Now I had the problem of what I was going to do with Bertha, who'd begun to nod in and out of consciousness. I needed him to answer my questions, and for that he had to be sober and awake. My only option, it seemed, was to take Bertha home with me. As foolish and risky as this proposition appeared, I felt I had no other choice.

Reeling under his weight, I propelled him back towards the main road. I had very little money left, and doubted that any cabbies in this neck of the woods would recognize me as Mr Bruff's office boy and offer to take my fare on account. But I had a plan. First I had to find a cab—easier said than done—then I had to convince the driver to take us back to the Cally Road, a distance of some few miles, in exchange for a bottle of port. In the end I had to throw in a Dundee cake as well, to sweeten what was already a very good deal.

'Oh, Octopus, Octopus!' moaned Bertha, as Julius helped me to lower him on to my bed-roll an hour or so later.

'Why is he calling you that?' asked Julius, his eyes fixed nervously on Bertha. 'And why is he wearing a dress?'

'Perhaps he's in disguise,' I suggested, hoping that this might satisfy his curiosity.

'It's not a very good disguise, Octavius.'

Looking down at the large, clumsy figure with the battered face, I could only agree. 'No, it isn't, is it? The truth is, Julius, Bertha thinks he's a woman.'

'But he's not a woman.'

'No, I know he's not. But just try to understand that *he thinks* he is.'

My brother took a moment to consider this. 'I'll try. I'm not sure it will work, though,' he added, as Bertha started to snore.

'Hungry?' I asked, and produced a second Dundee cake from my jacket.

'Starved!'

I cut two massive wedges and his smile became animated once more. As we ate, I quizzed him about the "panic word" I had drilled into him from a very early age. With Bertha in our midst, my former life was now too close for comfort.

'Do you mean "*Unnecessary*"?' he said, his smile fading fast. 'I don't have to write it again, do I?'

'No, no,' I reassured him, remembering every bungled attempt that had featured too many C's, and not enough N's or S's. 'I just want to be sure that you're clear about what you're to do if I ever use that word in your hearing.'

'I'm meant to run, Octavius. Run as fast as I possibly can.'

I smiled. 'And what are you supposed to do then?'

'Hide myself until night falls, then make my way back here.'

'And then?'

'Well, if you're not here, or if it's not safe, or if you don't return by morning, I'm meant to go to Gray's Inn Square and present myself to your employer, Mr Bruff.'

'And if anyone tries to stop you from entering the building?'

'I dash past them—whoever they are. I run up the stairs and find Mr Bruff's office, which is the one that's halfway along the corridor. I knock respectfully—unless I'm being chased, in which case I rush straight in.'

'And why do you knock respectfully?'

'Because Mr Bruff is an important man.'

'How important?'

'A *very* important man.'

'And what do you tell Mr Bruff?'

'I tell him that I am your brother Julius, and that something bad has happened to you. If he doesn't believe I'm your brother, I tell him to look at my eyes, for they should be proof enough.'

I beamed at him. 'Here, I have a present for you,' I said, and handed over the pencil.

'Oh, thank you, Octavius! I love it! What does it say?'

'It says "*Souvenir of the Thames Tunnel*".'

'Does that mean we have to do a word tonight?' He glanced uneasily at Bertha.

'No, it's late. You should get some sleep.'

Julius collected his bed-roll and laid it out as far away from Bertha as he could manage. I briefly considered falling asleep in my chair, but then thought better of it. I fetched my winter coat off the peg, spread it out like a rug in front of the door, and stretched out on top of it. If Bertha woke before me, there was no way he was getting out of there without waking me first.

In the event, I needn't have worried, for it was Julius who woke me when he was leaving for work. Bertha was also awake. He sat slumped over the table with his head in his hands, his cap and ribbons in a tangled mess. He glanced up at me as I joined him and let out a mournful groan.

''E's got your ogles' he said, gingerly tracing the cut on his cheek with the tip of his finger. 'Is 'e your brother, then? If he ain't, he ought to be. 'E's like this tiny, little you. Oh, Gawd, me head bleedin' hurts!'

'Who did this to you, Bertha?'

'That omi…the one wot calls hisself *"The Client"*.'

'What on earth did you do to make him beat you and chain you up?'

'I don't know, do I? Johnny sent me to give him a message, right? I give him 'is message—and everything's sweet—then all of a sudden he turns round and whacks me in the eek!'

'What message, Bertha?'

'Well, you know, just what you told me…how it's really the old lady wot's got the duggairiotype now. And I says, "It must be a damned good likeness, to go to all this trouble to get it back." Next thing you know, he whacks me in the eek!' Bertha sniffed. 'They're not always bona likenesses, see, and I knows that for a fact. You remember Pan-faced Dora? The palone with the mole, wot she claimed was a beauty spot?'

I was forced to admit that I did. There'd been a cruel, heartless saying about Dora's beauty spot, how it was in fact the only spot of beauty that Dora possessed.

'Well, each week Dora would put a little somethin' aside from her earnings and, when she'd saved up enough, she and 'er girlfriend went and got their pictures took. When she showed it to me, I couldn't believe me ogles. Dora's mole had upped and moved itself over to the other cheek! Never told her, mind. It would have had her spitting nails.'

'Bertha, I need you to be honest with me...was it you who put the daguerreotype in the old lady's hand-bag?'

Bertha sighed and shook his head. 'Of course it wasn't, Octopus. I was the one wot was meant to lift it, see? But I never got the chance. The mark must've ditched it in the old girl's bag, so, when I was pattin' her down, like, she never had it on 'er.'

'The mark?'

'The girl—the one we was meant to follow. The feelie palone wot was carrying the duggairiotype round with her.'

'Girl? What girl?'

He tutted. 'The one wot works as a lady's maid. She was the one that the Client hired us to lift it from.'

Lady's maid? Surely he couldn't be talking about Miss Penelope? No, it was unthinkable. And yet, when

I did think about it, it was the only way that this thing made sense.

Though I still couldn't quite bring myself to believe it fully, I was sure of one thing. Bertha was telling me the truth.

CHAPTER FIVE

'WHERE WAS YOU YESTERDAY?' George hissed in my left ear, as he trudged beside me down the corridor towards Mr Crabbit's office.

'Yes, where was you?' echoed his namesake in my right. 'We was made to run errands!'

'That's right. Errands. *All* of them!'

I thought about the different ways to respond to this—including (but not limited to, as Mr Bruff would have me add) the obvious, the fact that, as office boys, this was their job—but then it suddenly dawned on me. If I wanted to cause a reaction, why not tell them the truth?

'George, George, if you really want to know, yesterday Mr Bruff paid me to sit in a coffee shop and eat cake.'

'You was eating cake while we was running us-selves ragged?'

'Uh-huh.'

'And Mr Bruff was *paying* you?'

'Well, he will have paid me as soon as I claim back

my expenses,' I said. And, with that, I pulled my receipts from my pocket and knocked briskly on Mr Crabbit's door.

A crotchety voice called out, 'Enter!'

To rub salt into their wounds, I purposely left the door ajar as I strode into the petty-cash clerk's tiny sanctuary, so that George and George would be able to witness the transaction for themselves. As it turned out, this was a gross miscalculation on my part.

Mr Crabbit inspected each of the three receipts I handed him the way that a judge might when assessing the admissibility of evidence in a murder case.

'What's this, boy?' he demanded.

'It's a receipt for a pencil, sir. I had to buy a pencil in order to make some notes.' The way I saw it, I had bought the pencil for my brother out of my own pocket, and I was simply using the receipt in lieu of the one I had failed to acquire at the ticket booth.

'I can see it's for a pencil, boy. No, look again. Look carefully. What's this?'

'It's crumpled?'

He smiled and removed his spectacles. 'Yes, it's crumpled.'

'So?'

'Observe, boy.' Without turning to look himself, he raised a short, bony finger and pointed to the sign that hung behind him on the wall:

No illegible receipts
No indecipherable receipts
No torn receipts
No crumpled receipts

No defaced receipts
No stained or water-damaged receipts
No receipts with additions or alterations
No receipts requiring further explanation

A burst of muffled sniggering wafted through the doorway. Mr Crabbit rose like a whirlwind from his desk—no easy task for a slight, balding man of his particular stature—and pulled the door open as if he were about to rip it off its hinges.

'George and George. Why am I not surprised? Well? What do you require?'

'N-nothing, sir.'

'N-no, sir, nothing.'

'Then be about your business, both of you, before I report your idleness to Mr Bruff.'

Mr Crabbit shut the door in their faces and calmly returned to his desk.

Having collected my money, but only for the cake and the candle, I made my way upstairs to Mr Bruff's office. The Georges were perched on the bench outside. They scowled at me as I knocked and entered.

I was in two minds as to just how much of yesterday's adventure I was prepared to share with Mr Bruff. Without incriminating Miss Penelope directly—a thing that I wished to avoid until I'd had a chance to investigate her fully—it seemed prudent not to reveal too much. Too many facts were bound to lead to questions, and questions demanded answers—answers that I wasn't yet ready to give. Mr Bruff, bless him, was quite entranced by the dry and rather limited account of my movements, as I described how I'd traced the flower girl in question, followed her to a nearby pub noted for hosting bare-knuckled fistfights, then shadowed her as she made her way east as far as the Thames Tunnel, where, upon entering, she had managed to give me the slip. I summed up by saying that I was sure I could trace the girl again and that I had devised a plan for making her talk.

'Excellent work, Gooseberry,' said Mr Bruff. 'I really don't know how you manage it.'

It's easy, I thought. *I simply leave out all the important parts, such as the fact that the flower girl was actually a man who was currently moping about in my lodgings, too scared to set foot outside my door. He would happily whistle like a canary if he thought I might turf him out.*

Aloud I said, 'Sir, it occurs to me that the gang may attack again.'

It was almost certain they would, now that they thought Mrs Blake's aunt was in possession of the daguerreotype.

'You may be right,' he replied. 'I'll warn the Blakes to take extra precautions.'

'I think you should include Mrs Merridew, too.'

Mr Bruff grunted his assent. He took out a sheet of paper and began to scrawl a hasty note.

'George!' he called out at the top of his voice. I kept my eye on the door, curious to see which one of them would appear.

It was the younger of the two who answered the call. He glared at me mutinously as Mr Bruff instructed him to deliver the message and then, instead of leaving straight away, he hovered like a lump in the doorway. When Mr Bruff inquired about the delay, he turned a bright beet-red.

'Sir, why can't you send him?' he said, pointing his finger at me. 'George and me, we ran all the errands yesterday. Why can't he go this time?'

Mr Bruff raised his eyebrows. 'Gooseberry? That's out of the question. I require Gooseberry for other duties.'

'Like bleedin' eating cake,' George muttered.

'I beg your pardon?'

George scowled angrily at Mr Bruff and then he scowled at me. 'I didn't say nothing,' he replied at last, before deigning to leave the room.

For several seconds Mr Bruff sat staring at the spot where George had been standing. 'Would you believe that boy is only sixteen? The other one's seventeen, yet the pair of them waddle about like a couple of middle-aged men. I only have myself to blame. I should never have allowed them to become so slothful and obese.'

Mr Bruff rose, took a key from his desk drawer, and proceeded to open his office safe. He extracted the daguerreotype, dusted it off with his fingers, and placed it in his pocket.

'Come,' he said. 'We have an appointment with a certain gentleman in Hanover Square. I am hopeful that he will be able to identify the people in this picture.'

Again he requested my presence in the cab. As he was in an amiable mood, it seemed like a perfect opportunity to bring up the matter of my expenses.

'Mr Bruff, sir,' I began, 'last night I was obliged to take a cab home from Wapping. As I didn't have any money, I was forced to find an alternative method of payment.'

Mr Bruff stared at me. 'Octavius, please tell me that you didn't resort to stealing?'

'I didn't filch anyone's wallet, sir, if that's what you mean.' Which was true as far as it went. Mr Bruff looked touchingly relieved. 'But if I am to investigate this case,' I continued, 'in the manner you would wish me to…' I left it up to my employer to finish the sentence.

'Then you will require sufficient funds to enable you to move about the city at will. Yes, I can see that. I shall have a word with Mr Crabbit when we return to the office. He will provide you with an allowance by the end of the day.'

The cab turned off Oxford Street into Hanover Square and pulled up outside an impressive-looking building, which, Mr Bruff explained, was a rather exclusive gentleman's club. He also warned me that there might be a problem about my accompanying him in. There was. The man at the desk was quite adamant that on no account were children to be admitted to the Oriental Club. We remained in that polite state of impasse until Mr Murthwaite, the gent we had come to see, arrived and insisted that the three of us be shown to a private chamber, out of sight and out of hearing of any member who might object to my obviously troublesome and distressing presence. The man at the desk regarded me sullenly and called for one of his minions. I returned his look with a beaming smile as the underling led us away.

We were shown up to a surprisingly nice room, the

likes of which Mr Bruff might call "*well appointed*". It had a roaring fire down one end and prints of Indian scenes on the walls. Upon entering, Mr Murthwaite, a tall, lean man with skin the colour of mahogany, turned to my employer and clasped him warmly by the hand.

'It's been a long time,' he said.

'Too long, sir,' Mr Bruff replied. 'May I present Octavius Guy, one of my most trusted and valued employees, who, you may be interested to hear, was instrumental in unravelling the mystery of the Moonstone diamond?'

A pair of steady, attentive eyes studied me with interest. The gentleman whom they belonged to reached out and offered me his hand. 'It's nice to meet you, Octavius.'

'It's very nice to meet you, sir.'

'Mr Murthwaite is the celebrated Indian traveller, famed for his exploits in the East,' Mr Bruff explained.

'If we have time, I do hope you will honour me by relating your contribution to the Moonstone affair, for I had some small part to play in it myself. However, I believe Mr Bruff wishes to consult me on another matter first.'

'I do, sir.' My employer took the daguerreotype from his pocket. 'I wonder if you can cast any light on this?'

Mr Murthwaite opened the case and gazed at the photograph. For a minute he neither moved nor spoke.

'What is it you would like to know?' he asked presently.

'Can you identify either of these people, sir?'

'Certainly. During my time in India I was privileged to meet them both. The man's name is Login. Dr John Login. Solid sort. Dependable. The boy seated next to him is Duleep Singh, the Maharajah of Lahore, and leader of the deeply troubled Sikh Empire.'

'The boy's a maharajah?' I burst out, unable to hold my tongue. *Note to self: if you can keep your expression suitably blank when you're pocketing things, surely you can learn to control your tongue?*

Mr Murthwaite smiled. 'He most certainly is. He was barely five when he assumed the title. He would be about your age now, Octavius. I imagine this photograph was taken two or three years ago.'

'This Dr Login, is he some kind of adviser?' inquired Mr Bruff.

'In one sense, yes. Though it may be fairer to say that he is the boy's warder. It's a long story.'

'Sir, I would be much obliged if you will tell me anything you can.'

Mr Murthwaite nodded. 'Then we should sit.'

He herded us towards the fireplace and we took our seats around the fire.

'Duleep's father was the great Ranjit Singh, the Lion of the Punjab,' he began, 'who conquered the rival Sikh nations and forged them into one great Sikh empire. During the course of his life he took several wives, who between them bore him a total of eight sons. Only two of these were ever recognized as his legitimate offspring, however, namely Kharak, the eldest, and Duleep, the youngest, who was born barely a year before Ranjit's death in 1839.

'Naturally, it fell to Kharak to succeed him. But

within three months Kharak found himself brought up on charges of sedition, the most damning of which alleged that he'd been colluding with the British. You can bet your last cheroot that these charges were pure trumpery, for they were based solely on the rumours spread by one man—Ranjit's old adviser, the wazir Dhian Dogra, a deceitful wretch who had designs on the throne himself. Nevertheless Kharak was deposed and imprisoned, and died within the year, the victim of slow and gradual poisoning.

'It was Kharak's son, the nineteen-year-old Nau Nihal, who inherited the title on his father's deposition— though not for very long, as things turned out. He was struck by falling masonry while re-entering the Fort of Lahore, having just overseen his father's cremation. Though his companion was killed outright, Nau Nihal was merely wounded. The wazir Dhian had the unconscious ruler dragged inside, and then ordered the gates to be locked, so that none, not even his mother Chand Kaur, might enter the fort. By the time she was permitted to see him, a strange transformation had occurred. What was once a simple flesh wound had become a mortal injury. His skull had been cracked open and Nau Nihal lay dead.'

Mr Bruff threw me a nervous look. I think he was worried that the tone the story was taking was unsuitable for my young, delicate ears. Bless his naive, deluded soul!

'Chand Kaur now proclaimed herself as regent,' Mr Murthwaite continued, 'ruling in the place of Nau Nihal's as yet unborn son, for, as it happened, Nau Nihal's young widow was with child. Chand's brazenness so infuriated the wazir Dhian that he wrote at once to Sher Singh, son of Ranjit by his estranged first wife, urging him to muster his troops and march on Lahore. Sher Singh did as the wazir requested and, after the ensuing battle, Chand Kaur conceded defeat. She agreed to retire to her late son's palace on one singularly ill-conceived condition: that she receive a pension of a million rupees. It was a fatal error of judgement on her part. When her daughter-in-law gave birth to a stillborn infant—signalling the end of Kharak's blood-line and any further claim to power—Dhian replaced her servants with his own and had them club her brutally to death.'

'I say,' Mr Bruff interjected, 'remember the boy is listening!'

'Do not trouble yourselves on my account, good sirs,' I tried to reassure them both. 'There's nothing I love more than a good story, and the bloodthirstier the better, as far as I'm concerned.'

Mr Bruff nearly choked. Mr Murthwaite, on the other hand, burst out laughing.

'Then I shall try to make the climax as gruesome as possible,' he promised. 'Now, where was I? Ah, yes. Sher Singh. By all accounts the new leader was anxious to re-establish harmonious relations between all the feuding Sikh factions. He managed to broker approximately twenty months of relative peace, but then, one morning, while he was attending a friendly wrestling match on the outskirts of the city, he was lured to his death by a pair of brothers who'd been supporters of the late Chand Kaur. Sher had always had a fascination with weapons, so when they offered to show him their latest rifle, he readily agreed to accompany them outside. As Sher took the barrel in his hand to examine it, the first brother pulled the trigger and shot the maharajah in the chest. The second brother then took his sword and hacked off the poor man's head. That done, the pair rode away to Lahore, carrying the severed head with them. They tracked down the wazir and made him grovel at their feet, then placed the rifle to his temple and blew out his brains. Which is how the five-year-old Duleep came to rule an empire, although, of course, it was his mother who acted as his regent.'

'Extraordinary!' I cried, clapping for all I was worth, while Mr Bruff sat fuming.

Mr Murthwaite took out his cigarette case and extracted a cigarette, having offered Mr Bruff one first. He lit it, drew the smoke into his lungs, then blew it out again towards the ceiling.

'In December of 1845,' he said, 'Britain declared war on the Sikh nation, in what was to become known as the First Anglo-Sikh War. They—*or should I say we?*—won.' I sensed a touch of bitterness in his voice. 'Although they kept Duleep as the nominal figurehead, they imprisoned his mother, and subsequently sent her into exile. After the Second Anglo-Sikh War four years later, Britain annexed the Punjab, deposed young Duleep, and placed him in the care of Dr John Login. At first the two of them went to live in the fortress of Fatehgarh. I imagine they hoped that his followers would come to forget him. Out of sight and out of mind, and all that. In all likelihood, this photograph of yours dates from that particular period. 1849;

1850, at most. It can't be any later.'

'Why not?' asked Mr Bruff.

'Because although Fatehgarh was capable of holding a twelve-year-old boy captive with astonishing ease, it proved unequal to the task of containing his story. While Duleep remained on Indian soil, he would always inspire supporters. So last year they brought him here to England on the pretext of visiting the Great Exhibition. I know this because I saw him there.'

'So the maharajah's here? In Britain? Do you know by any chance where he is staying?'

'I may be on a nodding acquaintance with royalty, Mr Bruff, but I can hardly claim a place in his social circle. Dr Login, on the other hand, is quite another matter. I happen to know he's a member of this club. The secretary is bound to have his address on record. If I remember rightly, the chap runs some kind of hospital, somewhere out Richmond way. If anybody can tell you where the maharajah is, it is he.'

Mr Murthwaite smiled and stubbed out his cigarette. He closed the clasp of the daguerreotype and handed it back to my employer.

'Now, Octavius,' he said, as he turned to me, 'it's almost midday. Let us see how that damnable lackey who refused you entry likes it when I order us all a good, slap-up dinner.'

CHAPTER SIX

LUNCHEON STARTED OFF WITH a carrot soup that tasted very strange indeed. I'm not sure I liked it. Then came the main event, a dish of rice, which Mr Murthwaite called "*kedgeree*". He said that, although it was actually a breakfast food, he enjoyed it so much that he happily ate it at any time of the day. It took my mouth a little while to get used to all the competing flavours but, once it did, I found it was really quite more-ish. I didn't imagine it was something I could taunt George and George with, however. I had a shrewd suspicion they'd turn their noses up at rice.

By the time we got back to the office there was a reply awaiting us from Mr Blake. He expressed his thanks for Mr Bruff's concern and assured him that he would put measures in place forthwith to increase security at both his own and Mrs Merridew's residences.

Mr Bruff was true to his word and arranged for Mr Crabbit to provide me with a sum of money—a *per diem*, he called it—that I could use at my discretion, to be topped up each day as required. When I asked if I would need to provide receipts, Mr Bruff assured me that I would not, but I wasn't convinced that Mr Crabbit would see things the same way. So when he called me to his office to give me my seven shillings and sixpence—an extremely generous amount on Mr Bruff's part—I made sure I put the question to him as well. I half expected to see his finger point to the sign on the wall.

> *No illegible receipts*
> *No indecipherable receipts*
> *Etc., etc.*

Instead he shuddered a little, gritted his jaw, and said, 'No receipts will be necessary.' I'm not sure there wasn't a tear in his eye. 'But,' he added quickly, in a tone that sounded like begging, 'any receipts that you do provide will be gratefully received.' I almost felt sorry for him.

With the coins rattling happily around in my pocket, I set off homeward, stopping only to purchase three pork pies, a whole black pudding, and three bottles of ginger beer on the way. When I got to my lodgings, I was surprised to find the door locked. First I tried knocking. No response. Then I tried shouting.

'Bertha, it's Octopus! Open up!'

When that didn't work, I tried looking under the doormat for the key—for I'd given one to Bertha to lock up with, in the unlikely event that he needed to go out. There it was, damn the man! I still had a great many questions that needed answering and he was the only person in a position to enlighten me. I picked up the key and let myself in.

The room was exceedingly warm. Judging by the heat that was radiating from the stove, Bertha must have lit it just before he left. When I looked, I saw a puzzling amount of firewood stacked in the crate in the corner. There was two, maybe three times more than there had been that morning. I placed the victuals I'd bought for our supper on the table and went and stoked the fire, opening and closing the metal door with the handy makeshift tool we always use. I slipped off my jacket and sat down on a chair. I might have fallen asleep but for Julius arriving home.

'Octavius!' he shouted, as he ran to hug me. All at once he noticed the feast on the table. 'Black pudding! Ginger beer! And are those eel pies?'

'No, pork.'

'Well,' he said philosophically, 'you know I like pork pies, too, don't you?'

'I know, Julius, I know.'

Our reunion was interrupted by a sharp knock at the door. When I answered it, there stood Bertha, looking extremely sheepish.

'I hoped to get back before you did,' he said, bustling past me into the room, 'but I got stuck on the wrong side of the road and had to wait till all those damn cows had gone by. Look, I got us some potatoes,' he added. 'We'll cook 'em and 'ave 'em for supper.'

Julius's face fell.

'Bertha, I already got us some supper.'

Ignoring the spread on the table, Bertha knelt by the stove, grasped the poker, and began raking through the ashes in an unnecessarily elaborate fashion. He inserted the trivet and, taking care not to burn himself, placed three large potatoes on top.

'I won't have you thinking that I don't contribute nothing,' he mumbled, as he manipulated the stove door's catch back into place.

'What word will we do tonight?' piped up Julius, who'd been watching all this from his seat.

'I don't know…what word do you think will be useful?' I asked, grateful for the sudden diversion.

'How about "*welcome*"? As in, "*I know someone here who isn't*—"'

'Julius!' I barely managed to circumvent him in time. 'Can we talk about the word later, please? After we have supper?'

'Potatoes should take an hour,' growled Bertha, as he sat on the floor with his back to the wall, for Julius had piled the two remaining chairs with stacks of scrap paper.

That hour crawled by at a snail's pace. By the end of it, I understood one thing: this was not a flip-a-coin situation; scared or not, Bertha was *not* staying here.

We ate in silence, with Julius nudging his potato away from him till it was perched on the edge of his plate. Bertha took a bite out of his own one and suddenly burst into tears.

'How can I ever go back?' he wailed, the soft chunk of potato still swilling round his mouth. 'The Client's bound to peach on me to Johnny 'bout how I done somethin' wrong—though for the life of me I don't know what it was. And Johnny being Johnny, he won't 'esitate to punish me. Like as not he'll throttle me to death. Oh, wot am I to do? Wot am I to do?'

Julius had been in the throes of biting into his pork pie when Bertha burst out crying. He now sat frozen in that position, staring at the fully-grown man before him bawling and sobbing into his shawl.

'Johnny always had a temper—you know wot he was like—but when he took over from Ned, it just got worse and worse. He changed, Octopus. He changed…and not for the better. Set up his 'eadquarters at the Lamb and Flag—started running bare-knuckle fistfights out of there. Now they calls it the Bucket of Blood, and with good reason, too. Those fights are to the death; it's no holds barred with Johnny.' Bertha clapped his hand over his mouth to try and silence the great, heaving sobs rising from his chest.

'Bertha, what happened to Ned?'

'Oh, Octopus, the Yard nabbed Ned a good five years back. Hauled him up before the magistrate on some trumped-up charge of burglary. Claimed some old geezer got himself hurt while the job was going down, so everyone thought he'd swing for it. He didn't, but they did transport 'im off to Tasmania. Ned, though, he never done it. You know wot he felt about violence. There are some as say Johnny was behind it all—not to his face, o' course. Say it to his eek and he'd cut you to bleedin' ribbons.'

Bertha was still sobbing sporadically throughout this speech and Julius was still gawking at him. I wondered how much of this my brother understood.

Very little, I hoped, though even *very little* was more than I was comfortable with.

'Bertha, what can you tell me about the Client?'

''E's just some bloke wot Johnny knows. A regular at the fights, I think. Came to Johnny not long before Christmas, offering to pay him a king's ransom to get his bleedin' duggairiotype back.'

'What was he doing in the tunnel?'

'The tunnel's where he works.'

'Works?' My thoughts immediately turned towards the waiter.

'Not *works* like you and me works.' Bertha brushed the tears from his eyes with the heel of his palm. 'The Client's a toff, see. Sits at one of the tables. Sits there all day, treating it like it's 'is office. 'E wanted somewhere to base himself, like, till we got our 'ands on the picture, so Johnny suggested the tunnel. Just because 'e runs all the scams there, I reckon 'e's come to think of the tunnel as 'is.'

'But the waiter must be working for Johnny?' He had to be. There was no way on God's earth that he didn't know what his storeroom had recently been used for.

'Lots of 'em as work there do. They all know wot side their bread's buttered. Gawd, I wish I'd never gone and given 'im 'is message. And by now he'll have told Johnny all about me and, Johnny being Johnny, who knows wot the hell he'll do!'

No matter how much Johnny might be Johnny— no matter how sorry I might feel for Bertha—I couldn't allow him to stay here, not at the expense of my brother's peace of mind.

'Bertha,' I said, as gently as I could, 'I understand you'll need to lay low for a while, but after tonight I'm afraid you'll have to—'

I felt a sudden burst of pain as—under the table—a foot delivered a swift, nimble kick to my shin. Julius was staring at me with big, bulging eyes…well, eyes that were bulging even more than normal. When he saw that he had my attention, he gave an almost imperceptible shake of the head.

'Octavius,' he said, keeping his voice carefully modulated, 'can I have a word with you…outside, please?'

He rose and I followed. On the landing he pulled the door closed and, as there was no moon that night, we were left standing in total darkness.

'Octavius, he's really scared.'

'I know, Julius.'

'He's scared for his life.'

I nodded in agreement but said nothing.

'This man, Johnny, is he really as bad as he says he is?'

I didn't want to scare my brother, but I thought he deserved the truth. 'Yes.'

'Will he hurt him?'

'Probably.'

'Then we have to let him stay.'

I smiled, not that he could see it.

'Octavius?'

'Yes, Julius?'

'How do you know Johnny?'

I sighed. I had been dreading this question. For Julius's sake, I'd always kept my work and my private life separate. Even now that I was respectable, I still continued to do so. Mr Bruff had no idea I had a brother.

'Julius, do you remember our mother? Do you remember when she died?'

'I'm not sure. Sometimes I think I do.'

'You were very young at the time, so I had to look after us both. I had to make sure we had food and clothes, and somewhere to sleep for the night. Sometimes that meant I had to do things, things that I wasn't very proud of.'

'Bad things?'

Good question. 'Yes, bad things,' I said, and gave him a minute to let this sink in. 'Johnny also did bad things. At the start we used to work together.'

'Like you and Mr Bruff?'

'No.' *More like George and George*, I thought to myself. 'Mr Bruff's a good man…a very important man.'

'Would you have done bad things if our mother hadn't died?'

'Oh, Julius. I don't know. I certainly hope not.'

'Octavius?'

'Yes, Julius?'

'Why does Bertha call you Octopus?'

'It's the nickname I had when I first met him.'

'Who gave you the nickname?'

'A man named Ned.' He'd given it to me when he made me his deuce—his second-in-command—but I didn't think my brother needed to know that.

'Did Ned do bad things too?'

'Yes.'

'As bad as Johnny?'

'No. The things Johnny did were far worse.'

'Then we have to help Bertha.' Despite the dark I could sense him smiling.

'We do, don't we? Which one of us is going to give him the good news?'

'I know it should be you, because he's your friend, but I'd like to do it.'

We spent the remainder of the evening in far better spirits than those in which it had started. When Julius settled down to practise his word for the night—"*welcome*"—he loaned Bertha his old pencil so that Bertha could practise too. Bertha was at a disadvantage, for he didn't know his alphabet, but Julius took him in hand and taught him how to pronounce each of the letters. Soon it was time for bed. While Julius got himself ready, I took Bertha outside.

'You're welcome to stay here,' I told him, 'but heed this. The less Julius knows about my past, the better. Do you understand?'

He nodded.

'And another thing. The less my past knows about Julius, the better that is, too. When all this is over—when it's safe for you to go back to your old life—Julius will remain our little secret. You're to tell no one about him. All right?'

'Thieves' honour.'

That didn't inspire my confidence. As I knew only too well, there was no honour amongst thieves.

'Bertha, you would be wise never to cross me where Julius is concerned.' I don't know if it was the tone of my voice that impressed him, but when Bertha responded, he sounded petrified.

''Course. O' course, Octopus. Our secret. I understand.'

The next morning Mr Bruff received another summons from the Blakes. As our cab rattled its way down Oxford Street, I considered once more the tricky question of how much I should tell my employer. Again, I decided against telling him anything, at least until I got a chance to interrogate Miss Penelope myself. It was almost certain that she'd stashed the daguerreotype in Mrs Merridew's handbag. But if she had a good, honest reason for putting it there, why remain silent about it? Why not tell the Blakes what she had done? And how had she come to be in possession of a portrait of Duleep Singh in the first place? Had she *stolen* it from that shadowy figure who called himself the Client?

That particular gentleman, I reflected, was definitely worthy of closer investigation, for it wasn't the police he had turned to when it came to recovering the picture; it was the violent, bloodthirsty leader of a London-wide criminal gang. No, the Client was almost certainly more sinner than sinned against; that much was clear. But how had a lady's maid like Miss Penelope got herself mixed up with such a man?

As the cab drew into Montagu Square, I wondered if I was about to find out.

CHAPTER SEVEN

THE BLAKES' LIBRARY LOOKED much the same as it had done the previous Monday. Mrs Blake's aunt, Mrs Merridew, was seated in the middle of the room with an embroidery hoop in her hand. Mr Blake was no longer pacing; instead he was seated at the table with his wife. The fire was lit and, curled up in front of it, Mr Betteredge, the Blakes' elderly retainer, lay dozing. Betteredge's daughter, Miss Penelope, stood gazing out of the window at the street. Although she no longer looked like she'd been in a cat fight, the late-morning light revealed the tension in her face.

Mr Blake rose and shook my employer's hand. 'But where's the swiftest, slipperiest pickpocket in all of London?' he inquired. 'Is Gooseberry not joining us today?'

It occurred to me that either Mr Blake suffered from the most rotten eyesight or he'd been trained from birth not to notice his lessers.

'I'm here, sir,' I said, stepping forward with my bowler hat clasped behind my back—for once again it was Samuel who had answered the door to us, and once again he'd left me holding it. After Mr Blake made his usual fuss of me, I surreptitiously placed it on the seat of one of winged armchairs, where it was effectively hidden from view. There'd be no reproachful looks from Miss Penelope today.

'You're the goods, Mr Bruff! The very goods, sir,' waxed Mr Blake lyrically. 'I don't know how you foresaw this latest attack, but I'm very glad you did.'

'It was Gooseberry who alerted me that it might happen. What did happen, by the way? Your message only indicated that there had been another incident.'

'There was an attempt on my wife's aunt's house during the night. Thanks to you and Gooseberry, Mrs Merridew's steward was prepared for them. He managed to fire off three shots, which sent the beggars running.'

Mr Bruff turned to the old lady with a look of concern on his face. 'Mrs Merridew…how terribly distressing for you.'

'Not at all,' she replied. 'I wasn't even there. My niece, who is fully aware that I dislike explosions that go off in the night—pistol fire included—thought it best I come and stay with her. That way, in the event of an explosion, she would be on hand to comfort me.' She smiled at Mrs Blake, who rose from the table and went to pat her aunt's hand. 'What I don't understand,' the old lady continued, 'is what they were hoping to achieve.'

'I assume they were looking for the daguerreotype,' replied Mr Bruff.

'But that makes no sense whatsoever,' Mrs Blake

pointed out. 'Why would these bullies go to the trouble of planting the daguerreotype on poor Aunt Merridew, only to attempt to steal it back a few days later?'

I saw Miss Penelope's jaw begin to clench.

'It might make sense if what we were dealing with here was not one gang but two,' Mr Bruff suggested. 'Two rival crews competing over the same photograph—one desperate to conceal it, the other to retrieve it.'

Everybody regarded him doubtfully. Only Miss Penelope, who had balled her hand into a fist, remained looking elsewhere. As I watched, her knuckles began to turn white.

'Well, it's just a theory,' he sighed.

And a rather poor one, as theories go, for although there were hundreds of gangs in London, none of them were rivals. Instead they were structured along army lines, with all of them reporting to Johnny. If anyone tried to set out on his or her own, Johnny would quickly put a stop to it. Even Ned, despite his marked distaste for violence, was not beyond forcibly insisting that everyone kept ranks.

'I do, however,' my employer continued, 'bring news of the photograph itself. I have made some inquiries and have managed to identify the portrait's two subjects. The man is a Dr John Login, who, I am told, acts as the boy's guardian. The boy himself is Duleep Singh, the Maharajah of Lahore.'

As Mr Bruff paused for emphasis, I glanced about at people's faces. Everyone's mouths had dropped, including Miss Penelope's. Whatever her part in this, this was clearly news to her.

'The boy? A maharajah?' Mr Blake spluttered incoherently.

'Yes, although he was deposed by the British after the Second Anglo-Sikh War. I have reason to believe that he now resides in England, in the care of his guardian, who runs a hospital of sorts, out Twickenham way. I've written to the doctor, asking for an interview, and I await his reply. In the meantime, I think it might be safest if the daguerreotype remains with me.'

As there seemed to be little more to add, we started to take our leave. Having summoned Samuel to fetch Mr Bruff's hat and coat, Mr Blake turned to his wife and said, 'I am sorry to abandon you, Rachel dearest, but I have important speeches to write. I'll be tucked away in my study until dinnertime at the very least.'

'Then Aunt Merridew and I will take a turn around the square,' Mrs Blake replied.

'Are you sure that's wise? What if there's another attack?'

'Samuel can come with us. He's a fair shot with a pistol. You can handle a pistol, can't you, Samuel?' she added, as the footman returned with Mr Bruff's things.

'Most certainly, madam.' The footman fairly beamed at the prospect.

Mr Blake led us out into the hall; his wife and her aunt followed. I glanced back into the library, where I'd purposely left my hat sitting on the chair.

'Mr Bruff, Gooseberry, I wish you both a good day.' Mr Blake saluted us from the stairs as Samuel ushered us out.

We hadn't long to wait before we spied a passing

cab. Mr Bruff hailed it at once. As soon as it had drawn to a halt, he called out our destination to the driver and climbed in.

I hung back.

'Sir,' I said, as he held the door open for me, 'I seem to have forgotten my hat. I think I left it in the library. Please don't wait for me—I'll retrieve it and make my own way back.'

He nodded his assent and pulled the door closed, then signalled the cabbie to drive on.

I went and stood on the corner. Presently Mrs Blake's party emerged. Once they were safely in the distance, I sprinted back to the house and rang the bell. As I had hoped, it was Miss Penelope who answered the door.

'Gooseberry?' she said, gazing down at me. 'Is anything the matter?'

'I think I left my hat in the library, miss.'

'Wait here and I'll get it for you.' She went to shut the door in my face. I quickly put my hand out to stop it from closing.

'Miss Penelope, the truth is I left my hat here in order to get a word with you in private.'

'Indeed? With me? And why would that be?'

'Let me in, miss, and I'll explain.'

I would like to be able to say that her pale blue eyes were full of apprehension as she opened the door to me. In reality, they were only mildly curious.

I had imagined our interview would take place in the library, for that's the room we were always shown in to. Instead she stood her ground, forcing me to face her in the hall. Of all the rooms in the house, this was her domain. It was she and Samuel who ruled the roost here, deciding who would be granted entry and who would not.

'Now that you have my attention, young man, I think you had better begin.'

'First a question, miss. Between you, how do you and Samuel divide up the task of answering the door?'

Miss Penelope blinked. 'It normally falls to Samuel. But he'll warn me if he's going out, or if he's about to take his break, and then it falls to me. Why do you ask?'

Ignoring her question, I ploughed on. 'And when you were plagued with nuisance callers, miss, what was the routine then?'

Her mouth tightened. 'It was decided that only Samuel should answer the door.'

Another piece of the puzzle fell into place.

'Miss Penelope, I know the truth.'

'The truth?'

'I managed to locate the flower girl, miss, the one who was there when you were attacked. She admits to being hired, though not to plant the daguerreotype. She was there to steal it…from you. It was you who put the daguerreotype in Mrs Merridew's bag.'

Miss Penelope stared. 'And why would I do such a thing?' she asked.

'It's my belief that you were trying to protect it, miss.'

'Really?'

I nodded. 'This is what I think happened. When you no longer answered the door to them, the gang was forced to take stronger measures. They broke a window in the servant's quarters to gain entry to the house. Either by a stroke of luck, or, as I suspect, because you had already started carrying the photograph about with you on your person, they didn't find what they were after—hence their last ditch attempt to steal it from you in the street. You knew you were their target, and you knew that they would find it, so you took the one course of action left to you: you slipped it in the old lady's bag, where you hoped they wouldn't look.'

'I must say, you have a very vivid imagination.'

'You're right, miss, I do. For example, I *imagine* you expected to retrieve the daguerreotype once you were safely back home. But you'd been hurt and Mrs Blake insisted that Cook tend your wounds, so you never got the opportunity. Now, I don't *imagine* for one instant that you are a bad person, miss, so what I'd like to know is why you didn't then make a clean breast of things to the Blakes?'

As I gazed up intently into Miss Penelope's eyes, I saw the last thing I expected to see. A trace of a smile. She was *glad* to be rid of the photograph. She'd kept it safe from those who had plotted to take it from her and now she'd delivered it into someone else's protection.

Miss Penelope gave me a shrewd look and asked, 'Gooseberry, what do you want?'

'You've always been kind to me, miss. So I wanted to give you the chance to tell me your side of the story before I put the matter to Mr Bruff.'

'Then we're done here.' She made a move towards the door.

'Please, Miss Penelope, I beg you. Tell me how you came by the portrait. When Mr Bruff revealed whose portrait it was, you were as astonished as anyone. That makes me think that though you needed to keep it safe, you had no idea of its significance.'

'Gooseberry, it's time for you to leave.'

'Who is the Client, miss? And why does he want it so badly?'

'I don't know! I don't know!' she cried, losing her temper at last. 'Now, go! Leave this place!'

'Please! You must answer my questions if you want my help!'

Just then the door to the library opened and her father, Mr Betteredge, stepped into the hall. He was carrying my hat.

'What is going on here?' he asked, studying both our faces in turn. 'Why all the shouting?'

Miss Penelope took one look at her father and burst into tears. Beating a retreat, she fled up the stairs to one of the floors above. Mr Betteredge came forward and held out my hat.

'Yours, I believe,' he said, and handed it over. 'Young man, while it is true that I have never entirely understood my daughter, in my heart I know her to be a good and honest girl. I will not stand idly by to see her upset by the likes of you.' He nodded thoughtfully as he hobbled to the front door. He pulled it open and stood waiting for me to take my leave.

Although I'd told Mr Bruff I would return to the office, I now had a change of plan. When one door closes, it forces you to go knocking on others. Since Miss Penelope refused to tell me what she knew, I had no other choice but to hunt down the Client myself. So, with my seven and sixpence jangling in my pocket, I headed south towards the pier at Hungerford Bridge.

Steamboats for Greenwich departed from here twice hourly, making a number of stops along the way. On inquiring when the next one was due, I discovered that I had twenty minutes to spare, so I went and bought myself a spot of dinner—a bun with a great slab of cheese in the middle and a bottle of ginger beer to wash it down. I took it back with me to the pier, then settled down to wait. Before very long I was boarding the steamer with the other passengers and, as the boat pulled noisily away on its slow journey eastward, I found a seat with a decent view of the river and tucked hungrily into my bun.

It's not often I get to travel by boat, so it felt like an adventure. I soon found myself regretting not having brought my winter coat along, however. The freezing, damp air whipped frenziedly about me, chilling me to the bone. I began to stroll around the deck, searching for somewhere to take shelter. Failing to find anywhere suitable, I went and sat down again.

'Tunnel Pier!' came the captain's cry at last, when my earlobes had lost all feeling. 'Disembark here for the Thames Tunnel!'

It seemed that most of my fellow travellers were bound for the same destination. I joined the queue at the gangplank and simply followed the herd through the streets. Soon the pale-grey marble tower came into view and people started queuing all over again.

Having paid my penny, I descended the stairs and

made directly for the coffee shop. Business was even brisker than it had been on Tuesday, and people were obliged to share tables if they wanted a seat. That made my task infinitely harder. I had counted on identifying the Client by looking for a gent sitting alone at a table. But nobody was seated alone.

I stepped back into the shadows and kept my eye on the waiter. After ten minutes, I began to see a kind of pattern to his movements. As tables emptied and tables filled, he would take people's orders as he cleared the dirty crockery, then would presently return with their chosen cakes and drinks. After thirty minutes, he'd worked his way around the entire floor, serving every single person…bar one.

The gentleman in question was a man in his late twenties, pale of complexion, with dark hair and a beard. He was seated at a table with a group of three women, all of whom he patently ignored. He passed the time by reading his newspaper and making notes in a small pocket diary. The cake and the glass in front of him remained untouched. Having found my target, I just had to wait.

'The Tunnel is closing in fifteen minutes. Please make your way to the exits!'

Now timing became everything. As he rose, I passed by his table, and for the merest instant my arm brushed his. He looked up, but by then I'd already gone, dodging into the crowd before circling back to follow him. Up the stairs he went and out through the exit, with me in hot pursuit. He turned right and stalked up to the main road, then headed west past the docks and the Tower. He was going at a rollicking pace, forcing me to put on a burst of speed every now and then to try and keep up. At Aldgate he turned left and took the turning into Leadenhall Street. Throngs of people crowded the pavement, homeward bound after a long day's work. One second I'd lose sight of him, only to glimpse him again the next.

Then—I'm sorry to say—I lost him for good.

I looked around and took my bearings. Leadenhall Street was the heart of London's financial district, where commodities from all over the world were traded and deals were struck that could make or wreck entire nations. All its grand buildings smelled of money and profit, and it was into one of these that the Client had escaped.

Retracing my steps, I hailed a cab. The cabbie looked annoyingly sceptical till I showed him the colour of my coins. I climbed into the carriage, then sat down and removed the Client's diary from my pocket—well, you knew I'd lifted *something*, and you surely can't imagine it was his newspaper! I opened it to the very front.

"*Property of Mr Josiah Hook, Esquire*," it said. So now the Client had a name. "*If found, please return to Room 219.*"

As I prepared to take my first ever ride in a cab on my own, I turned the page.

CHAPTER EIGHT

MR HOOK—*ESQUIRE'S*—DIARY was only helpful to a point. As he had started it on New Year's Day, there were only twenty-two entries in total. Each of these was made in small, cramped writing, and most featured items of news copied from newspapers, such as "*Royal Mail's* Amazon *burns and sinks in the Bay of Biscay*" or "*Transvaal receives its independence*"—various goings-on from around the world, with all the place names underlined twice.

Every Tuesday, Thursday, and Saturday was marked with the letters "*BOB*", followed by a set of figures that obviously referred to an amount of money. Some days the amount recorded was positive, some days negative. This stumped me at first—in fact to begin with I assumed "*BOB*" was a name—but then I realized all the labelled days were Covent Garden market days, when the Bucket of Blood held its bare-knuckle fights. Mr Hook, it seemed, liked a bet. Presumably this was how he'd met Johnny in the first place.

The parts that will be of greater interest to you (and

the parts that were of greater interest to me) were even harder to make sense of, for all were written in abbreviated script, like this snippet from January 1st:

"*Our recs. show Thos. Shep. Broth. in service Port. Pl. res., name of Jas. Have J. F. M. set watch on ho. in case Thos. left port. w/ Jas.*"

By working backwards from incidents I could identify, I was eventually able to expand it to this:

"*Our records show that Thomas Shep*[herd?] *has a brother in service at a Portland Place residence*—Mrs Merridew's residence, on the face of it—*who goes by the name of James. Have Johnny Full Moon set a watch on the house in case Thomas left the portrait with James.*"

As far as I could tell, this whole affair had started with Thomas, an unknown entity, who'd given the daguerreotype to his brother, James, for safekeeping. Though not a betting man myself, I'd wager two pairs of brand new boots that this James was the footman who, claiming the need to tend to his sick brother, had given Mrs Merridew his notice.

Had Thomas stolen the portrait from Hook? Though this was unclear, there was one thing I was certain of. He'd gone to extraordinary lengths to make sure Mr Hook did not get it back. The daguerreotype was obviously the key to this business.

But how had Miss Penelope come by it? Two identical entries on Sundays 4th and 11th provided a tantalizing hint:

"*Jas. S. meets girl Rgnt's zool. gards. monk. ho. 2.30 pm.*"

Translation:

"*On both dates, James Shep*[herd?] *met a girl*—Miss Penelope, given the nature of later entries—*in or by the monkey house at Regent's Park zoological gardens at 2.30 pm.*"

She'd been seeing James on her afternoons off, and quite regularly it seemed. When Johnny's lot was sent to deal with him, James had given her the portrait to look after before quitting Mrs Merridew's service.

There was one entry that especially worried me—the penultimate one, as Mr Bruff would have me call it:

"*Freak escpd. Tell J. F. M.: need to be dealt w/ termin. Entry into Port. Pl. res. set for tonight.*"

There wasn't a chance in a million that the escaping freak could be anybody but Bertha. But why, exactly, was it necessary that he be dealt with *terminally*?

What was it Bertha had said? 'I give him 'is message—and everything's sweet—then all of a sudden he turns round and whacks me in the eek!' What had caused this sudden fit of rage? What had Bertha seen or done to make Mr Hook want him dead?

I was in two minds whether to tell Bertha about this. In the end I thought it best he be warned, so I broached the subject with him as soon as Julius left for work.

'Looks like I'll need a disguise, then,' was his only response.

When I got to the office that morning, I barely had a chance to top up my *per diem* before Mr Bruff was calling for me. Within minutes we were outside in the square, climbing into a cab.

'This came this morning,' he said, handing me a letter as the cab rumbled south towards the Strand:

Cole Park Grange Asylum,
Twickenham.
January, 22nd inst.

Sir,

With reference to your recent inquiry, I regret to inform you that Dr Login is currently abroad and will be incommunicado for the foreseeable future.

However, if you would care to visit, I am happy to place myself at your disposal if you think I can be of help to you in any regard.

Your humble servant,
Mr Cyrus Treech,
Director in Dr Login's absence.

'Sir, what do you hope to achieve by seeing the doctor's second-in-command?' We were crossing Waterloo Bridge at this point and the cab had just pulled up at the toll gate.

'Perhaps he will be able to throw some light on this,' he replied, pulling the daguerreotype from his pocket.

My heart sank. I knew by now that possessing the portrait was dangerous and the fewer who knew that he had it, the safer he'd be. But how was I going to warn him of this without telling him what I'd found out?

'Mr Bruff,' I began, 'after we parted yesterday, instead of returning to the office I went to follow up a lead I'd been given. It turns out you were right: there *are* two rival gangs at work here.'

'I knew it!' he cried, elated to have his lamentable theory vindicated.

Well, in a sense, it *was* true after a fashion. I slowly went through the whole story for him, substituting the word "*gang*" for any involvement by Miss Penelope, the footman James, or Thomas, James's shadowy brother. Mr Bruff listened attentively as we boarded our train at Waterloo. He was still listening attentively as we sped our way westward towards Twickenham.

On arrival there, we were told that Cole Park Grange Asylum lay within walking distance from the station. The winter air was clear and crisp as we crunched our way along the gravel path. Soon we came to a pair of wrought-iron gates set into a high brick wall. Inside the gates there stood a tiny hut, where a guard was stationed on duty. Mr Bruff stated our business and the man let us in.

Cole Park Grange Asylum was a sprawling two-storied building set in several acres of grounds. Some attempt had been made at landscaping, though there was nothing as formal as an actual garden. Rather, the sweeping lawn was broken up in places by an occasional tree or a small clump of shrubs. To my mind, it made the estate look windswept. On the journey up to the house, I counted five of the doctor's patients standing about on the grass, looking for all the world like they too were part of the design.

On entering, we were shown to the doctor's study and told that Mr Treech would join us presently. Before very long, the door opened and a gentleman in his late forties entered the room. His face was clean-shaven, his hair was brushed back, and his eyes gleamed warmly behind a pair of wire-rimmed spectacles. His skin was deeply tanned—not quite as dark as Mr Murthwaite's, but he'd certainly seen the sun quite recently—and he was dressed rather finely in a well-cut suit. He came forward and gave Mr Bruff's hand a hearty shake.

'Welcome, sir, to Cole Park Grange.' He seated himself behind the large mahogany desk. 'I am Mr Treech, Dr Login's assistant. Perhaps you have come to see the good works we do here? As you're no doubt aware, Dr Login is a specialist in ailments of the mind—delusions, sir, feeble-mindedness, and despair.'

'Mr Treech, my name is Bruff.'

'Ah, Mr Bruff! Of course! You wrote requesting an audience with the good doctor. Unfortunately he's away travelling—somewhere up near the Prussian border, I believe. But perhaps I can be of assistance?'

'The matter we are here on is a delicate one, I fear.'

'Indeed?' A look of inquisitive bemusement appeared on Mr Treech's face. He tilted his head to one side.

'I have been led to believe,' said Mr Bruff, 'that Dr Login acts as guardian to the Maharajah of Lahore.'

Mr Treech smiled. 'Yes, that is quite correct.'

'I wished to inquire about a certain daguerreotype that was made—a portrait of the young maharajah, with Dr Login at his side. It recently came into the possession of a client of mine in a highly unsatisfactory manner.'

'Unsatisfactory?'

'*Highly* unsatisfactory,' repeated Mr Bruff, refusing to go into detail.

'Do you have the portrait with you?'

I glanced at my employer, wondering if I'd managed to persuade him of the threat that the daguerreotype posed.

'No,' he said, after a moment's pause, 'I have deposited it with my bank for safekeeping.'

Mr Treech shrugged. 'Then I'm afraid I cannot help you.' As Mr Bruff and I rose from our chairs, he suddenly raised his hand. 'But perhaps there is someone here who can.'

'Who?'

'Why, His Highness himself, sir. The Maharajah of Lahore.'

'The maharajah is here?'

'Not in the house, no; this building is reserved for patients. The maharajah resides in the doctor's private quarters, which are located elsewhere on the grounds. I can take you to him, though I can't guarantee he will see you. His Highness is a very private person.'

'We would be indebted, sir.'

Mr Treech led us down a passage and out through a door into the stable yard at the back.

'Before its conversion into a hospital,' he explained, gesturing to the delivery of vegetables we could see being made at the kitchen door, 'this house used to have its own tenant farmers. Although no longer tied to us directly, they still keep us supplied with fresh produce. Dr Login believes that the first requirement of a healthy mind is a healthy body. We serve only the best, nutritious food to our patients.'

We rounded the stable and followed a rutted dirt track, which brought us to another set of gates. Beside them stood an old gatehouse that had small leaded windows, roses round the door, and a low trellis fence at the front.

'Dr Login had the interior refitted before he moved in. It is truly most charming inside. If you will please follow me?'

He opened the gate, walked up to the door, and knocked. After a brief interval, a young man appeared. When he saw Mr Treech standing there, he held the door open and ushered us in.

'How is His Highness today?' Mr Treech inquired, as we all removed our hats.

'Fair to middling, sir,' the young man replied, taking Mr Treech's and Mr Bruff's, but leaving me with mine. *Oh, the joys of being a social inferior!* 'At the moment he's practising his letters.'

'Will he receive us, do you think?'

'I couldn't rightly say, sir.'

'Well, we can but try.'

We followed Mr Treech up the stairs, to a doorway halfway along the corridor at the top. He tapped softly and waited. Upon receiving no reply, he gingerly pushed open the door. I edged my way in between him and Mr Bruff, so I too might see what they could see.

At the far end of the room, a brown-skinned boy of my age was seated at a table. Light from the window fell sideways across his face, casting one side of it into shadow. He had been in the process of writing something, for a dip-pen was poised in his right hand. He regarded the three of us thoughtfully, before at last settling on Mr Treech.

'Why do you disturb me?' he asked, his warm, sultry

voice almost singing out the words.

'Your Highness, this gentleman is Mr Bruff. He wishes to beg an audience.'

The boy studied my employer for a moment. Then he smiled. 'No, I will speak with him,' he said.

He was pointing at me.

I thought Mr Bruff might have an apoplexy, but instead he put his hands on my shoulder and propelled me gently into the room.

'Your Highness,' Mr Treech protested, 'this is highly irregular!'

'I have made my decision,' the boy replied. 'If you worry for my safety, you may, of course, leave the door open…as I am sure you will.'

He placed his pen on the table and rose, then came forward to greet me. 'Welcome,' he said, offering me his hand. 'What is your name?'

'Octavius,' I said, tucking my hat under my left arm, then grasping his hand and shaking it, 'though most people call me Gooseberry.'

'Gooseberry? What an odd name. And yet it suits you. Where do you live, Gooseberry?'

'In London, sir. Just off the Caledonian Road— near where they're building the new railway terminus.'

'A railway terminus? How very fascinating and modern. Come. Come and see what I am doing.'

He led me to the table and offered me a chair. Resuming his seat, he turned the sheet of paper around so I could see it. Written repeatedly in flowing script was the phrase: "*Duleep Singh, Maharajah of Lahore, former leader of the great Sikh Empire.*"

'I am learning to write your English,' he explained.

'You write it very well, sir,' I said, and he smiled. I wanted to tell him that I was teaching my brother to write, but that would have involved talking about Julius in Mr Bruff's hearing. Instead I settled for a partial lie. 'I teach my neighbour's boy,' I explained. 'Each night I give him a different word, and he sits and practises it.'

'Oh? And how is that going?'

'Honestly? Very, very slowly, though he always tries his best.' I could feel Mr Bruff's eyes on me, willing me to move on to the subject of our visit. 'Your Highness, we have come to ask you about a portrait you had made, a daguerreotype that has recently come into our possession—'

'No! We will talk about writing English! Give me a word!'

'What?'

'Each night you give your neighbour's boy a word. Give me a word and I shall write it.'

I scratched my head. 'What word do you think will be useful?'

'"*Sovereignty*",' he said at last, 'since I no longer have sovereignty over my own people.'

'Sovereignty?' I wasn't entirely certain how to spell it myself. Then I realized it was probably like *seven* and *seventy*: *sovereign*—the head of state, our gracious queen and, perhaps most importantly, a one pound coin— with a -*ty* tacked on the end.

He offered me a fresh sheet of paper. I dipped his pen in the inkwell and began to write out the word. As I slid it back across the table, I wondered what Julius would make of this term, with its tricky vowels that could all too easily be transposed, and its "*ign*" just begging to be written as "*ing*".

I studied the lad's face as he wrote. He was as handsome in real life as he was in the photograph, his flawless skin only marred by the short, angry-looking scar that ran from the far corner of his right eye down to the top of his cheek.

'There,' he said, dashing off the "Y" with a flourish, 'how is that?'

I rose from my seat and went and peered over his shoulder.

'You've transposed the "I" and "E",' I said, and he looked up with a frown. 'This letter here and this one here…they should be the other way round.'

As I bent down to point them out, he unexpectedly whispered something in my ear:

'When you go, leave your hat behind. Trust me. I promise to return it.'

His eyes met mine and for the briefest instant they burned intensely. Aloud he said, 'This is a most difficult word. I will need to practise it. Sit.'

Aware that I was still being watched from the doorway, I casually propped my hat upon a chair, the back of which I judged would hide it neatly from view. That accomplished, I went and sat down again. For five minutes the boy worked in silence. Then he placed his pen on the table in front of him, and looked up and smiled.

'I have enjoyed your company, Gooseberry, and I thank you for teaching me a new word. But now I should like to rest.'

I rose and gave a little bow, then turned and walked

towards the door. Just as I reached it, however, Mr Treech cleared his throat.

'You've forgotten your hat,' he said.

'Oh, yes…so I have,' I agreed unhappily, and went to retrieve it. As I picked it up, I noticed the boy. The features had frozen on his face. Then he rallied a little. He stood up and walked towards me.

'It was a pleasure to meet you,' he said, and reached out to shake my hand again. I could feel the tension in his body; his shoulders were perfectly rigid. And then he suddenly relaxed. As I turned to go, I even thought I saw a smile.

The man who had opened the door to us was waiting to show us out. He fetched the two hats he had taken and handed them back to their respective owners. We were just on the verge of departing when the young maharajah came bolting down the stairs.

'Gooseberry,' he said breathlessly, 'I believe that you dropped this.'

In the palm of his hand was my handkerchief, embroidered with the letters "O. G.". I got an overwhelming feeling that Mr Treech would have snatched it from him then and there, had such an action not seemed wildly inappropriate.

'Isn't that the one I gave you for Christmas?' asked Mr Bruff, who was also peering at it with interest. He seemed pleased to see that I was actually using it, and hadn't yet consigned it to the rag and bone.

'It is, sir,' I replied, as the boy pressed it into my hand. The question was, how on God's earth had he come by it? I'd certainly had no cause to take it out during the time I spent in his room. Which only left one possibility, as implausible as it might sound. The Maharajah of Lahore was a pickpocket. A pickpocket just like me.

I also had a good idea why he'd returned it, for through its folds I could feel the unmistakable texture of paper. The thieving maharajah had used it to smuggle me a note.

CHAPTER NINE

'GOOSEBERRY, COULD YOU NOT have pressed the subject of the daguerreotype further?'

Mr Bruff and I were walking back towards the station. The maharajah's note, if indeed that's what it was, was still concealed within my handkerchief, safely inside my pocket. Though I was burning with curiosity, I wanted to be alone when I examined it. Until I knew its contents, I wouldn't be able to judge whether this was something I wished to share with my employer— or, at least, share with him just yet.

'Mr Bruff—'

'No, no, you're right,' he said, now arguing the case for me himself. Isn't that just like lawyers? 'I'm being unfair. The maharajah clearly forbade you to talk about the photograph. I see that. And I can't think of anything I could have done in your position that might have changed his mind. Come. I think we both deserve a good dinner after all that. Let us see if we can find ourselves a place that serves a decent meal.'

After inquiring at the station, we set off towards

the river in search of the establishment that had been recommended to us.

The Jolly Boatman was a public house that commanded a fine view of the Thames, but apart from the occasional passenger-carrying wherry, there was very little river traffic to be seen. When I asked why, Mr Bruff explained that this stretch of the Thames was so far inland that it was no longer tidal, which prevented larger vessels—those that could only sail on the high tide—from navigating it.

Being the dinner hour, the place was busy, but we still managed to secure a table near the fire. Mr Bruff ordered the pea and ham soup for us both, with cheeses and chutney to follow. He had a glass of white wine, while I opted for a bottle of ginger beer. As soon as the publican had taken our order, I casually rose from the table.

'Call of nature,' I explained in response to Mr Bruff's unspoken query. Quickly catching the publican up, I asked and received directions to the W. C.

I made my way outside and followed the cinder track, as I'd been told to do, which brought me to a fenced-in yard at the rear of the building. Along the far wall stood a short row of water closets.

I entered the nearest one and bolted the door. Though I really *was* anxious to use the facilities, my call of nature could wait, whereas my curiosity could not. I pulled out my handkerchief and extracted the scrap of paper. It was a message, all right. In a hastily written, almost scrawled, cursive hand, this is what it said:

"Do not let Treech get his hands on the photograph. He

will destroy it, and the maharajah will be put to death."

I read it through several times. The first sentence seemed clear enough, even though the word "*photograph*" was a last minute substitution after the writer had tried and failed to spell the word "*daguerreotype*". It was the second sentence that worried me. *He will destroy it, and the maharajah will be put to death.* As much as I hated to share information with my employer—at least until I fully understood its significance—this was far too important to keep to myself.

A steaming bowl of soup was awaiting me when I returned to the table. I sat down with every intention of showing Mr Bruff the maharajah's message, but then something happened. I noticed a man standing in the doorway and recognized him as one of the guards from Cole Park Grange. He spotted us and casually took a seat at the nearest table. For the hour or so that followed, I managed to steer the conversation, quickly sidetracking Mr Bruff whenever I felt he was about to mention the case. Anyone watching or listening would have thought we were having a great old chat— and in a sense we were, for the meal was good, the company spirited, and the surroundings tolerably fair.

I thanked Mr Bruff for the dinner as we walked back to the station. I wasn't surprised to see that the guard was following us; what surprised me was how extremely inept he was at the job. Can you believe he stood a mere five feet away from us on the almost empty platform? I began to wonder if he had plans to board the train with us when it arrived. In the event he didn't. Having seen us enter a carriage, he simply waited where he was, and only turned to leave when the train pulled away.

'Sir,' I said, now that we were finally alone together, 'did you see that fellow who followed us from the Jolly Boatman?'

'What fellow, Gooseberry?' Mr Bruff may be an extremely astute lawyer, but sometimes his powers of observation fall pitifully short of the mark.

'The one with the pointy ears, sir. He was the guard on the gate at the asylum—the one who let us in. I think Mr Treech sent him to spy on us.'

'Spy on us? What possible reason would Mr Treech have to spy on us?'

'I think he wanted to find out if the maharajah slipped me a message.'

'Slipped you a message? That's absurd!'

'But, Mr Bruff, he did slip me a message. It was wrapped up in my handkerchief. Here, look…' I pulled the scrap of paper from my pocket and handed it to my employer.

His eyebrows rose considerably as he read it through. 'But what can this mean?' he asked.

'Sir, the boy went to a great deal of trouble to get this message to me. I didn't drop my handkerchief; he stole it from my jacket—and with all the skill and daring of a natural pickpocket, I might add. Now, unless he's referring to himself in the third person, the same way our good queen favours the royal "*we*", that leaves only one possible explanation, as far as I can see. The maharajah we met is an impostor.'

Faced with this brilliantly constructed piece of logic, I'm sorry to say that Mr Bruff remained singularly unconvinced. He opened the daguerreotype and held it up to the light of the carriage window.

'We know that this is a portrait of Duleep Singh, the Maharajah of Lahore. How do we know this? We have Mr Murthwaite's testimony to the fact. Two or three years may have passed since this picture was taken, but I'd be willing to bet that this is the same young man that we met today.'

I studied the flawless skin, several shades darker than my own. I noted the perfect, white teeth and the bright, soulful eyes, marred only by the short, livid scar on the right. I had to admit it: it certainly appeared to be the same lad.

Yet how did this square with the maharajah's ability as a thief? The boy was good at it, for when he took my handkerchief, I didn't feel his hand inside my jacket. If only he could learn to control the tension in his body, one day he might even be as good as me. One thing was clear, though: he was no novice pickpocket—he'd done it before. So when exactly had picking pockets been part of His Highness's lessons?

'How do you explain the handkerchief?' I asked.

'Very simply,' said Mr Bruff. 'It's just as the boy said. You must have dropped it.'

I knew I hadn't, but with Mr Bruff stubbornly refusing to believe me, it seemed futile to press the point. 'What about "*the maharajah will be put to death*", then? Who writes about himself in the third person?'

'Maharajahs, for all I know. And please don't tell me you know otherwise, because you're no more an expert on Sikh culture than am I. No, Gooseberry, these flights of fancy simply will not do.'

'Sir,' I tried one last tack, 'at the very least, you

must concede that this note suggests the maharajah's life will be forfeit if Mr Treech gets hold of the daguerreotype?'

That pulled him up short.

'Yes…yes,' he agreed reluctantly. Then he appeared to cheer up a bit. 'It does seem to fit with what we've discovered about the rival gangs. I suppose it is *just* possible that Mr Treech is in league with one of them.'

The wrong one, of course; not Miss Penelope and her sweetheart, who had both tried to keep the portrait from falling into the wrong hands. No, this gang was made up of mad Johnny Knight, Josiah Hook, and now—it would seem—Cyrus Treech. But why did they want the daguerreotype so badly?

'Sir, the portrait is key to this affair. What do you intend to do with it when we get back to London?'

'I think it would be best if I deposited it with my bank.'

'Then may I please examine it one last time?'

'Certainly.' He handed over the case.

I examined the scar again carefully, but couldn't find fault with it. It seemed identical to the one I'd just seen.

'Gooseberry, what in God's name do you think you're doing?' screeched Mr Bruff, as I used my thumbnail to slit the thin, paper seal down the edge of the glass. 'I order you to desist at once!'

All I was doing was prying the photographic metal plate out. I just wanted to see if there was anything hidden beneath it—some secret papers, perhaps, or even a treasure map. A treasure map would have been perfect. Unfortunately there was nothing of the sort.

'You had better be able to put that back in one piece, young man, or, so help me, I'll tan your hide till Sunday!'

'Look...look, Mr Bruff. It simply slots back into place. See? No harm done. Honest.'

'Hmmph!'

On our arrival at Waterloo, Mr Bruff was true to his word. He hailed a cab and we made directly for his bank in Lombard Street. While I waited for him in the carriage, my thoughts turned again to Mr Hook, for Leadenhall Street, where I'd last set eyes on him, was just around the corner.

When I reached home that evening, I found Julius and Bertha sitting at the table together, engaged in some kind of lesson.

'Nah, you got to say it quieter, Julius,' Bertha was explaining. 'Say it like you got the consumption eating away at yeh and you won't last to see another day. Cough a little. Wipe those bona, big ogles like you're brushing away tears. You wants to get their sympathy, see? Now try it again.'

'Varder me bona, fat eels, missus,' whispered Julius, coughing right on cue. 'Wouldn't you love to get your 'and round—'

'Rand! Rand! Didn't no one ever learn you to talk proper?'

Julius blinked and tried again. '*Rand* one of these whoppers?' he mimicked, undoing years of hard work on my part.

'Better. Now a few tears—no, don't go bleedin' overboard—yeah, that's it. Bona! If that don't get 'em buying up the whole damn barrel, nothing will!'

'What are you two doing?' I asked.

'I was just helping young Julius 'ere work up 'is patter.'

'His patter's just fine, Bertha.'

'But he tells me they don't let him serve on the barrow. All he gets to do is gut fish all day. A shame, that's wot I call it. Waste of good talent.'

'If you want to help him, then teach him something useful.'

'There ain't nothing more useful than a good line of patter.'

'I'd say that totting up a bill and making the correct change ought to come a close second, wouldn't you?'

'Wot? The lad don't know his money?'

'I do too!' Julius protested. 'I know all my coins by sight.'

'I know you do, Julius. But if Bertha's serious about helping you, he'll teach you how to add up and give change.' Anything had to be better than "*Varder me bona, fat eels, missus*". And who could tell, maybe Bertha would succeed where I had failed?

Bertha looked thoughtful. 'We could do with some proper money to practise with,' he said.

'Funny you should say that,' I replied, and delved into my pocket for a handful of my *per diem*.

Saturdays are unusual in that they may or may not be workdays, depending upon your station in life and also on your chosen profession. For Julius, it's his busiest day, and he's often not back from the fish stall until it's well gone midnight. For me, it very much depends on the whims and wonts of Mr Bruff. For

Mr Brutt, it depends on the whims and wonts of his clients. While businesses that sell things will most likely be open, the more successful and profitable those businesses are, the fewer the staff that will be in attendance—for men of wealth tend to flee the capital on weekends, preferring to breathe the superior quality of air that their country houses provide. A perfect day, in other words, to tackle the little project I had in mind.

First I needed to purchase a gift of sorts. I briefly considered buying a rat in a cage, but realized in time that such an odd offering would stick out in the memory. No, this had to be something inconsequential, and something that wouldn't cost me a fortune, for I also had plans for the Sunday.

After much deliberation, I took myself off to a rather select stationer's in Bishopsgate and picked out two nicely-bound pocket diaries.

'That will be one and six,' said the woman, when I took them up to the counter.

'Can you wrap them for me, please? In separate packages?'

'Why, certainly,' she replied, and set about parcelling them up in paper and string as deftly as a butcher wraps meat.

I gave her my best beaming smile. 'Do you by chance have a business card?' Of course they did; this was a *select* stationer's and their prices were outrageous.

'We do.'

'May I have two, please?'

'Two?' The woman frowned.

'I'd like to recommend this shop to my employer,

you see.'

'Of course.' She handed me two cards. 'Will there be anything else?'

'I'll take a pencil. And, oh,' I added, with a sudden burst of benevolence towards Mr Crabbit, 'may I please have a receipt?'

Leadenhall Street was only around the corner. Today there was a lot less traffic and the pavement was practically empty. I found the spot where I'd last seen Hook and paused for a moment to study my surroundings. I was searching for the street's most impressive building, and there was one less than thirty yards away that towered head and shoulders above the rest. Quite literally. It might easily have been a palace. I wandered along to the entrance—which was set behind a portico of towering Greek columns—and ran my eyes over the doors. They were standing open.

'Can I help you?' a man's voice called out.

I climbed the steps and poked my head inside. The person who'd hailed me, a jovial, bearded chap in his late fifties, stepped forward. He was dressed in a sumptuous uniform of red and gold livery.

'I have some parcels to deliver, sir, but as I'm new to the area, I'm not sure that I've come to the right place.'

'This is East India House, lad, the premises of the East India Company.'

'Oh, good.' I certainly hoped it was good.

'Who are the parcels for?'

'The first is for a certain Mr Josiah Hook, esquire, of Room Two-nineteen. Is Mr Hook here today?'

'Bless you, no, he won't be back till Monday. It's

generally just us porters on a Saturday.'

'Is Mr Hook your gaffer, then?' Since the man was only in his twenties, it seemed incredibly unlikely.

'My gaffer? Heavens, no! He's merely one of Sir Humphrey's junior clerks.'

'Sir Humphrey?'

'Sir Humphrey Mallard. A director of this esteemed company.' Bingo! Here was the man who pulled the strings. Somebody obviously sanctioned Hook's informal little office in the Thames Tunnel—which was far better suited to meetings with London's criminal fraternity than these hallowed halls—and who more likely than his boss?

'*A* director?' I queried. 'Why, how many directors are there?'

'Twenty-five in total if you count the board's chairman.'

I tried to look suitably awestruck. 'And what does this esteemed company do?'

'Do? Why, it makes money, lad. Lots and lots of lovely money.' The porter burst out laughing, leaving me none the wiser.

'Sir, the second parcel's for a certain Mr Thomas Shepherd, esquire, of Room…of Room…'

'Two-twenty—but Mr Shepherd hasn't worked here since before Christmas.'

'Oh, dear! What on earth am I to do with his package?' I asked.

'I don't rightly know what you should do with Mr Shepherd's, but you can leave Mr Hook's with me. I'll see that he gets it.'

'I'll need you to sign for it, sir,' I said, hugging it to

my chest as if I were about to protect it with my life.

Again the porter laughed, and readily agreed to sign. I took out my pencil and the two cards, which I kept sandwiched together so they looked like one. On the back of the bottom card I'd already written the words: "*One pocket diary to be delivered to Mr Josiah Hook, Room 219. Received, Saturday, January 24th, 1852.*" As it failed to mention the name of Mr Hook's workplace, I could have used it in any number of buildings up and down the street; it just so happened that I didn't need to, having struck gold on my very first attempt. What I actually wrote on the top one was, "*Compliments of the East India Company*"—not that the porter could see it.

I handed him the prepared receipt, and as he read it through and appended his signature, I slipped the one I'd just written inside the brown paper wrapping. When Mr Hook opened it and discovered the card, he'd be less likely to question where the diary had come from. I gave the porter the package and bid him good day.

So now I had a fourth name to add to my list. Sir Humphrey Mallard, a director, no less, of the East India Company. A man who made lots and lots of lovely money. I hasten to point out, lest I appear anything but entirely truthful on the matter, I also had a very nice diary for Julius. And another pencil. What I didn't realize at that point, as I exited the building, was that I was—at that very moment—being watched.

CHAPTER TEN

SUNDAY IS A DAY of rest—for the carriage class, at least. For their servants it's a different matter, though even they can expect a few sweet hours in the afternoon to conduct their lives in a manner of their own choosing. By a happy coincidence, Sunday is also the only day that my brother officially has off, so it's the one day of the week when we get a chance to do things together. He was going to love what I had planned for him for today: "*Jas. S. meets girl Rgnt's zool. gards. monk. ho. 2.30 pm.*"

Julius was overjoyed when I told him. So, unfortunately, was Bertha.

'I ain't never been to the zoo,' said Bertha, his face lighting up at the prospect.

'Neither have we,' said Julius, ''cos it ain't cheap to get in.'

'*Isn't cheap*,' I corrected him. 'Bertha, it's not a good idea for you to come with us,' I added.

Bertha's face fell. ''Course not, 'course not,' he mumbled. 'It ain't cheap to get in.'

'It's not the cost I'm worried about.'

'No? Wot, then? Wot you bleedin' worried about?'

I didn't want to say that Miss Penelope might be there, and that I was hoping to spy on her—at least, not in front of Julius. I had to settle for: 'The lady's maid you were following, it's possible she might try to meet someone there today. She could recognize you, Bertha.'

'Not if I was in disguise, she couldn't.'

'Disguise?'

'Turn round, both of you. You don't want to be gawking at no lady while she's undressing!'

We did as Bertha requested and both of us averted our gaze. Two minutes went by, punctuated by rustlings and the occasional grunt.

'All right, you can look now.'

Julius's eyes were popping out of his head. I expect mine were too. There stood Bertha, looking extremely uncomfortable in a blue serge jacket and a pair of matching trousers. He'd hidden his long, brown hair under the rim of a docker's flat cap. Since I knew Bertha had no money to speak of, I dreaded to think how he'd come by this get-up.

'Wot d'ya think?' he asked nervously.

I was so used to seeing Bertha in a dress, that, for a moment, I couldn't speak. In one sense, he still looked like Bertha; in another, he didn't.

'You look like a man,' said Julius.

'Uncanny, ain't it? Gawd, I never thought I'd be reduced to doin' drag.'

'It's the perfect disguise, Bertha.'

'So I can come?'

'I'll need to use the coins you've been practising with…but, yes. You can come.'

'But if you take 'is coins, how will young Sprat ever learn his money?'

'Young *who*?'

'Young Sprat here.'

Young Sprat beamed his approval at his new nick-name.

'I'll replace them tomorrow,' I promised.

Though Miss Penelope wasn't due until two-thirty (if in fact she was going to come at all), we set off early in order to make the most of the day. We walked up to the Thornhill Bridge, then took the steps down to the canal path below. There'd been a frost during the night and the grass beneath our feet was crunchy, as it was only just now beginning to thaw.

'You want to steer clear of that place,' muttered Bertha, as we passed the grim-looking workhouse on our left. We all stared at it and shivered, as if its very presence chilled the air.

'Come, let's move on,' I suggested.

We followed the cut as it curved its way through open fields, calling out to any lock keepers we knew by sight and waving at the narrowboats we encountered. Normally Julius would have attempted to pat the horses that pulled these barges along—a practice that on occasion had landed him in trouble with their owners—but today he ignored them, his mind clearly on things to come. He even ignored the railway yards that lay beyond the wharves at Camden, where we'd spent many a happy Sunday watching trains pass by.

When we finally reached the zoo gates, Julius could

scarcely contain his excitement. He was practically dancing a jig as we lined up outside the ticket hut. I fished the money out of my pocket—God bless *per diems*—and started counting out what we needed. Bertha saw what I was doing and laid his hand on my wrist to stop me.

'Why don't you let young Sprat do that?' he asked.

Doubtful of the outcome, though figuring it couldn't hurt, I held out the coins for my brother.

'How much is it?' asked Julius.

'A shilling each,' replied Bertha, peering at the only part of the sign he could read.

Julius stared at my palm so hard, it felt like he was trying to read my fortune.

'Come on, Sprat,' urged Bertha. 'You can do it. Just keep rememberin' who needs wot.'

'One for you,' he said, picking out a shilling piece and glancing up at Bertha. 'And one for you,' he said, choosing another for me.

There was a least one more shilling in my hand, but it was partially hidden by the pennies. When I went to uncover it with my finger, Bertha slapped my hand away.

As the seconds dragged by, the tension became unbearable.

Suddenly Julius's face lit up. 'And one for me,' he said, unearthing the silver coin from the pile of coppers. 'Three shillings, one for each of us.'

Julius handed the money to the man in the hut and received his three tickets in return. He looked as if he might faint with joy. I briefly wondered how Miss Penelope could afford an expensive outing like this on a weekly basis, but then realized that, unlike us, she didn't have to shell out for her food and lodgings. Even the coal for her fire was paid for. Every penny she earned was hers for the spending and, like servants everywhere, she had precious little time to spend it in.

'See, Sprat? Told yeh you could do it.'

'I really did it, didn't I?' He threw his arms around Bertha and gave him a huge hug.

We started down the long walkway in high spirits. They were soon extinguished when the only animals we saw were cattle and horses grazing in the field on our right.

'I seen enough damned cows to last a bleedin' lifetime,' growled Bertha, referring to the ones he'd encountered along the Cally Road.

'Look!' cried Julius, pointing in the distance. At the end of the path, half-hidden by the dozens of people gathered there, was a bear climbing up a pole. 'Quick,' he said, and started running towards it. Bertha and I glanced at each other, then set off running too.

As we got closer, it became apparent why the bear was climbing. The crowd was supplying him with fruit and cakes, which his keeper passed to him on the end of a stick. Sometimes he dropped them into the pit below, where they were quickly snapped up by one of the other bears.

When we finally managed to pry Julius away, we discovered a wealth of different creatures just around the corner—pelicans, leopards, raccoons, and wolves.

'What are they?' asked Julius, staring in wonderment at a herd of bizarre-looking animals with tiny heads and arms, but huge tails and feet.

'The sign says "*Kangaroos*". According to this, they're native to Australia.'

'Do you think they make good pets?'

I sincerely hoped they didn't.

'Gawd, to think that Ned looks out 'is window and sees *them* every day of his life!'

It was a sobering thought.

By one o'clock we'd worked up quite an appetite, so I bought us some buns and a slab of veal and ham pie each. The sun had come out, so we sat on the grass to eat, watching the llamas as they careered about their pen. I was able to keep an eye on the time, for there was a clock on the roof of their stable. The afternoon wore on. By two-fifteen we'd positioned ourselves out of sight on the far side of the monkey house, which afforded us a view of the entrance, but only if we peered round the corner. I began to question the wisdom of this approach, since three heads poking around the side of the building was bound to draw attention, especially as Julius had begun to whisper, 'Is that her? Is that her?' about every young woman he spied.

'This isn't going to work,' I told them. 'Bertha, why don't you take Julius back to see the zebras?'

'But, Octopus, I want to help. So does Sprat here, don't yeh, Sprat?'

Julius gave a violent nod of agreement.

'Then we need a way to get out there in the open without being noticed.'

'I got an idea,' growled Bertha, grabbing me and Julius by the arm and spinning us around till we had our backs to him. Then he prodded us together till we stood shoulder to shoulder. 'Concentrate, you two! You're a couple of feelies, see—?'

'We're what?' gasped Julius.

'Young lads, young lads,' he snapped. 'I'm your beloved father—right?—and all three of us is havin' a nice day out at the zoo.' Pulling us closer, he clapped one large hand over the left side of Julius's face, effectively shielding it from view. He then clapped his other over the right side of mine. Blinkered like this, I suddenly understood what it felt like to be a cart horse. 'I'm just showing me boys the sights, yeah? Wot could be more natural than that? Ready?'

He steered us out on to the patch of ground in front of the entrance, and not a moment too soon, for even with my restricted view of the world, I could see Miss Penelope approaching.

'It's her,' I whispered to try to warn Bertha.

'I see 'er,' said Bertha, already turning us to face another direction.

'What's she doing?'

'She's talking to some skinny cove in the doorway. 'E looks like 'e ain't ate or slept for a week.'

'How does she look?'

'Like a palone in love. Damn it! They're goin' inside.'

I felt a sudden pressure on my cheek. 'Bertha, what are you doing?'

'Shush! I'm gettin' us in there with them. How else will we hear wot they say? Just you relax and let me guide yeh. Remember, we're a family—right?—out seeing the sights.'

In this respect, Julius was far more adept at playing

the part than I was. As soon as he set eyes on the monkeys, he became entranced. He kept pointing out one gibbering primate after another as Bertha moved us ever closer to Miss Penelope and James. Eventually the pair came into earshot and I finally got to hear James speak.

'What happened to you last Sunday?' he demanded in a petulant voice. 'Why didn't you come?'

'James, the house was under siege. I couldn't get away.'

'Under siege?'

'From the same people who were pestering you at Portland Place, I think.'

'Oh, Penelope! I never imagined for a moment that they'd connect you to me. You don't know how sorry I am to put you through this. But the photograph, it's safe?'

Miss Penelope remained silent.

'For heaven's sake, Penelope, tell me it's safe!'

'It's safe enough.'

'What do you mean?'

'James, they broke into Montagu Square. They searched my room, but luckily they didn't find it. From then on, I had no choice but to carry it about with me—which would have been fine—but on Monday Miss Rachel insisted I accompany her to Mrs Merridew's. They ambushed me in the street.'

'No! Darling, were you hurt?'

'Just my pride, James—but, honestly, it was awful.'

'It weren't so bleedin' awful,' muttered Bertha. 'I seen a damn sight worse than wot she got.'

'Bertha! Shhh!'

'I knew that if I kept hold of it,' Miss Penelope continued, 'they'd be bound to find it on me, so I slipped it into Mrs Merridew's handbag. Fortunately, they didn't look there.'

'Oh, thank God. And you managed to get it back afterwards?'

'That's the problem, James. I didn't. Your old mistress discovered it before I had a chance to.'

'*What?*'

'She found it in her bag and was so perplexed by it that she had Miss Rachel call her lawyer.'

'No! No, no, no! How could you let this happen?'

'James, I had no choice! I could hardly claim it was mine and, if I told the truth, it would have meant involving you. You have no idea what it cost me to hold my tongue. Miss Rachel is not merely my employer, James; we grew up together, she and I. We were playmates when we were children. Oh! How I loathe abusing her trust!'

'Curse it and damn it to blazes!' His outburst set off the nearest group of monkeys, who started screeching and clambering about. 'Oh, let me think, let me think! Where is the daguerreotype now?'

'With Mr Bruff, Miss Rachel's lawyer. In all likelihood, it's safer in his care.'

'*Safer?* What if these people go to him and say, "Actually, that photograph's mine"? What if he simply *hands* it to them? What then?'

'Please do not adopt that tone of voice with me. I was only trying to help.'

'You don't seem to understand, it's not just the boy's life that's at stake!'

'*Boy*? He's no mere a boy, James. Oh, yes! That's right! I *know*! He's a maharajah, no less. Did it not occur to you to mention that fact to me when you enlisted my aid?'

There was a brief, awkward pause before James replied grumpily, 'I was trying to protect you, Penelope.'

'Protect me? How? By keeping me in the dark?' I could practically hear James scowling. 'Just what has your brother got himself mixed up in, I ask myself?'

'Thomas may be overly ambitious, but deep down inside he's a good man! When his guvnor approached him and asked for his help, he saw it as a way to further his career. Then he discovered just what that help would entail: he was to keep the boy and his guardian captive, to clear the way for an impostor to impersonate the maharajah.'

'To what purpose, James?'

'He's not sure. As the junior clerk with least seniority, he wasn't privy to his guvnor's scheme. He was kept in the dark about most things, an easy matter for his boss to arrange, since he and his prisoners were stuck on their own in some remote farmhouse out Twickenham way. He certainly didn't realize they planned to murder the boy; he thought they just needed him out of the picture until the day after the reception.'

'What reception?'

'Some special function they're hosting at Thomas's work. Look, I know he's been an idiot—my brother would be the first to admit it—but, honestly, as soon as he got wind of what they were up to, he tried to do the decent thing. He took the boy and his guardian and went into hiding.'

'And the daguerreotype? How does that figure into this?'

'According to Thomas, it's the only proof that the lad they have working for them is an impostor. While it survives, there's still a chance that he can be exposed for what he is. But if they manage to destroy it, then...'

'Then what, James?'

James sighed. 'No one is safe. Not me, not Thomas, and certainly not the maharajah. Perhaps, Penelope, not even you.'

So the maharajah—the *real* maharajah, that is— was now in hiding, beyond the reach of Treech and his cronies. Was the boy who was posing as him aware of the fact? I rather thought not.

'If the photograph's proof,' Miss Penelope went on, 'why didn't Thomas use it weeks ago and expose these people and their horrid plans?'

'Because he doesn't know what it's meant to prove— or how it's meant to prove it. The only reason he knows that it's proof at all is because his colleague happened to joke about it when he entrusted him with the portrait. Oh, I bet they're kicking themselves that they didn't get rid of it when they had the chance.'

'So where is Thomas now?' Miss Penelope's question was greeted by silence. 'James?'

'I don't know,' he said at last.

'You don't know...or you don't want to tell me?' More silence. 'Oh, let me guess,' she continued, her anger rising and setting off another bout of shrieking from the monkeys, 'you're just trying to protect me again!'

'Penelope, wait! Where are you going?'

'Home, James. I'm going home. I find myself tiring of all this unsolicited protection!' She stormed out.

James ran after her, but when he caught her up, she shrugged off his restraining hand.

'Bertha,' I said, 'stay here with Julius. I'll be back in a moment.'

I set off after James, who was standing motionless by this point, staring at Miss Penelope's retreating figure. Bertha was right; the man looked to be in really bad shape. His face was gaunt, his sandy-blond hair had not been brushed, and three days of prickly stubble adorned his prominent chin. His dull, glassy eyes barely registered my approach.

'What do you want?' he asked, once he realized I'd been gazing up at him for more than a minute.

'I wants yeh to know wot we'll do when we get our 'ands on that duggairiotype,' I growled, doing a passable imitation of Bertha, though my voice was obviously nowhere near as deep. 'We're gunna cut that dear, sweet girl of yours. Cut 'er up into shreds, we is.'

James paled. 'You'll leave her alone,' he gasped. 'It's me you want, not her. I swear she knows nothing.'

Then he added, 'Oi! Where do you think you're going?' as I raced to take cover behind the nearest tree, for coming down the path were two of Johnny's men. I didn't recognize them *per se*, as Mr Bruff might put it; I simply recognized the type. Despite the modest finery of their attire, they stuck out a mile from the crowd—two young men on their own amid the endless parade of courting couples and family groups. I kept watch to see if they would make a move on James, but they seemed perfectly content just keeping him under surveillance. James also must have noticed them, for within minutes he'd given them both the slip.

The fact that Miss Penelope adored James had been clear to me from the outset. And now I was sure that James loved Miss Penelope, too.

CHAPTER ELEVEN

'HOW ARE THOSE EYES of yours doing, Gooseberry?' inquired Mr Grayling, the infuriating junior clerk who bestowed on me my nickname. 'Either of them popped out of your head yet?'

Not so far, Christopher, but I'm sure they would, if you were ever to produce an intelligent thought.

I headed for Mr Crabbit's door and knocked.

'Enter!'

'Good morning, sir,' I said, as I slipped into the room.

'What's this, boy?' he asked.

'A receipt, sir. For two diaries and a pencil.' I swear there was a tear in the old man's eye and foolishly imagined it could only be from gratitude.

'I expect you have come for your *per diem?*'

'If it pleases you, sir.' He cast me a look to demonstrate just how much it pleased him, but he counted out my money nonetheless.

'Undoubtedly you will have heard about the fire?'

'If you're speaking of that terrible blaze last night,

sir, I think the whole of London saw it.' Julius, Bertha, and I had joined our neighbours down on the street, watching as the horizon lit up like a Roman candle. Although it was a chilly evening, it wasn't long before lanterns and chairs were brought out, then food and drink was passed round and jokes were traded about the chances of a building catching fire on Burns' Night. I really couldn't have wished for a more exciting end to a perfect Sunday—and one I expect Julius will take with him to his grave.

'Then I presume you will appreciate the need to spend conservatively at this time,' said Mr Crabbit, as he handed me the coins, '*and* I shall require a valid receipt for every single purchase.'

'Sorry, sir, I don't follow…'

'We hold a small reserve of cash in this office for contingencies, and that shall have to last us until the bank can arrange an emergency line of credit.'

'The bank?'

'Mr Bruff's bank, boy.'

'What about Mr Bruff's bank, sir?'

'Last night it burned to the ground.'

I dashed out of there like it was me who was on fire, sprinted past Mr Clueless Grayling—who was occupying his time by lobbing crumpled balls of paper at his fellow clerks—then bolted up the stairs as quick as I could. Abandoning my normal practice of knocking, I threw open the door and ran in.

Mr Bruff sat slumped in his office chair, his features drawn and grey. 'I can't bring myself to believe it,' he said, looking up at me. 'To destroy a single photograph, they burn down an entire bank? Tell me it isn't true.

Tell me the blaze was just a coincidence. Tell me I'm imagining things—just don't tell me I'm right!'

'Mr Bruff, I think we both know it was no coincidence,' I said, closing the door on the Georges, who, having been woken by my sudden arrival, were now trying to peek through the crack. 'First you inform Mr Treech that you deposited the daguerreotype with your bank, then two days later your bank burns to the ground. That sounds like a classic case of cause and effect to me.'

Mr Bruff let out a wail. 'To think I liked that man! And now that they believe the daguerreotype is no more, I suppose they'll go ahead and kill the maharajah—and it'll all be my fault!'

'They *believe* it's no more?' I queried.

Shamefaced, Mr Bruff rose and crossed the floor to his safe. 'Last Friday, as I was waiting in line to be served at the bank, I started thinking: what if Gooseberry's suspicions were just figments of the boy's vivid imagination? What if he wrote the note himself? What if Mr Treech was exactly what he seemed to be: an honest, congenial man? Fearing that I was over-reacting by depositing the photograph, I returned it to my pocket and brought it back here to the office.' He pulled open the safe door and extracted the slim, leather case. 'Now I feel I have no choice but to take the matter to the police.'

'Mr Bruff, you can't!'

'Let Scotland Yard deal with these rival gangs! Let them be responsible for protecting the maharajah!'

'Mr Bruff, I'm begging you. This is not something you want to do.'

'Gooseberry, I have no wish to discuss it further. I have made my decision.'

'You *cannot* involve the police in this, sir.'

'Why ever not?'

'Because one of those gangs is not a gang. It's Miss Penelope.'

Mr Bruff's eyes, which had shrunken into his head, suddenly grew wider. 'Miss Penelope?' he stammered. 'Miss Rachel's maid?'

I nodded. 'If you bring the police into this, they'll find that she was the one who put that daguerreotype in Mrs Merridew's handbag. She was trying to keep it from falling into the wrong hands, for it's the only proof that the boy we met is not the Maharajah of Lahore—though how it proves it, I really cannot say. For the moment, however, the real maharajah is safe… at least, I believe him to be. He's in the care of a Mr Thomas Shepherd, brother of one Mr James Shepherd, Mrs Merridew's former footman and Miss Penelope's Sunday sweetheart. As far as I can tell, Dr Login is with them too.'

Mr Bruff blinked and rubbed his chin. 'How long have you known this?' he asked.

'Honestly? I've known about Miss Penelope's part in it for some time. I didn't inform you because I knew you would wish to confront her, and I wanted to give her the chance to tell me her side of the story. The rest of it I only discovered yesterday.'

'And that's everything? You're holding nothing back?'

I put on my *offended face*, knowing that my *honest face* wouldn't suffice. 'Why should I hold anything back, sir?' I demanded, perfectly aware that I'd made no mention of Josiah Hook and Sir Humphrey Mallard, or the East India Company connection to the case.

'Gooseberry, even if I don't call in Scotland Yard, I do have a duty of care to tell my clients what I know.'

'The Blakes? But if you tell the Blakes, sir, they might sack Miss Penelope.'

'True. And they'd be well within their rights to bring the police into it themselves.'

'But, Miss Penelope…she was only trying to help.'

'I am not insensitive to her position, Gooseberry, yet I still believe the Blakes deserve to know.'

'Then let me be the one to tell them, sir.'

On the cab journey there, Mr Bruff hemmed and hawed most of the way, and twice he had to stop himself from asking me to explain it all again. Awkwardly, it was Miss Penelope who answered the door to us. This time, I'm sorry to say, her pale blue eyes *were* full of apprehension. She could hardly bring herself to look at us as she showed us to the library, and appeared to be on the verge of tears when she went to fetch the family. If Mr Bruff had had any doubts about the veracity of my statement, after a minute in her presence, they melted like spectres in the sun.

'Mr Bruff, are you sure we should do this?' I asked, as soon as she'd departed.

'Octavius, we must. You may wish to leave out the part about the bank, of course. It makes me look rather…rather…'

'I'll leave out the part about the bank.'

Mr Blake arrived first, followed shortly by his wife.

'Penelope is just collecting Aunt Merridew,' Mrs Blake explained as she took her seat. 'They should be along shortly. I take it there have been developments?'

'Of a sort, Mrs Blake, of a sort,' my employer replied. 'Gooseberry has discovered something that I feel you should know.'

'Really? Ah, here comes my aunt now.'

Miss Penelope helped the old lady to her chair, bobbed a brief curtsey to her mistress, and went to leave the room.

'If Mrs Blake has no objections,' said Mr Bruff quickly, 'I would prefer Miss Penelope to remain.'

The determinedly impassive mask dropped from the poor girl's face. Suddenly she appeared frail and wretched.

'I beg your ladyship's pardon,' came a voice from the doorway, 'but if my daughter is to stay, then I should like to be present, too.' Mr Betteredge, the Blakes' elderly steward, cast a severe look in my direction as he entered the room. I noticed he was carrying his copy of *Robinson Crusoe*.

'Well, now that everyone is here,' Mrs Blake said pleasantly, 'why don't you begin?'

'Before I start, miss,' I requested, 'I'd like to ask Mr Betteredge to share with us whatever passage he's been reading from his book.'

The old man gave a triumphant cry and, with great deliberation, opened the volume at a page about three-quarters of the way through. He cleared his throat and, in a tremulous voice, read, "'*As for the maid, she was a very honest, modest, sober, and religious young woman; had a very good share of sense; was agreeable enough in her person; spoke very handsomely, and to the purpose; always with decency and good manners, and not backward to speak when any thing required it, or impertinently forward to speak when it was not her business*".' He closed the book with a thump and looked up. 'When it was not her business,' he repeated.

Mr and Mrs Blake looked distinctly puzzled, as did Mrs Merridew. Mr Bruff closed his eyes and started massaging his eyelids with his thumb and forefinger. Miss Penelope stood by the door, tears streaming silently down her cheeks.

'Thank you, Mr Betteredge, sir,' I said, meeting his frosty stare. 'I will try to bear that in mind when I say what I have to say.'

'Come on, Gooseberry,' urged Mr Blake. 'Out with it! All this suspense is killing us.'

'Very good, sir. I am going to tell you a story. There are some aspects that I'm still not clear on, but it starts with a plot to replace Duleep Singh, the young Maharajah of Lahore, with an impostor—and then do away with him and his guardian, Dr Login.'

Mrs Merridew gasped. 'The boy in the portrait?'

'Yes, miss. The boy in the portrait you found.'

'But why would they wish to replace him?' asked Mrs Blake. 'What did they hope to achieve?'

'I've been giving that a lot of thought, miss. I *think* it's because the boy they replaced him with has skills.'

'Skills?'

'He's a common thief, miss,' I replied, though I thought, given the context, it best not to add "*like me*"—not that I'm in the least bit common. But then, if I'm going to be honest, neither was the boy I'd met.

135

'Gooseberry, how do you know this?'

'When Mr Bruff and I went to see the lad on Friday, he filched my handkerchief from inside my jacket, miss, in order to smuggle me a note. The note said, "Do not let Treech—"'

'Treech?'

'The man who seems to be in charge of Dr Login's asylum. He's definitely one of the ringleaders, though I don't think the boy is a willing accomplice. I think he's being coerced into it.'

'Go on.'

'Well, the note said, "Do not let Treech get his hands on the photograph. He will destroy it and the maharajah will be put to death."'

'Hold on,' said Mr Blake, 'you're telling us the plot failed? The real maharajah is still alive?'

'Yes, sir. You see, their plan was only *partially* successful. One of the conspirators, a certain Mr Thomas Shepherd—', I heard a sharp intake of breath from the doorway, '—baulked at the idea of killing a child. So he spirited the maharajah and his guardian into hiding, and took the one piece of evidence that could prove the impostor was an impostor.'

'The daguerreotype…'

'Yes, sir. The daguerreotype, which he gave to his brother for safekeeping.'

Mrs Merridew stirred in her seat. 'So how did *I* come to be in possession of it?' she asked.

Miss Penelope, who at this point seemed all cried out, raised her eyes and stared at me. 'If you're going to tell them, then get on with it,' she said, raising frowns on everyone's faces, for it was not the place of servants to speak so directly.

'You must understand,' I continued, 'that Thomas Shepherd is a man who made bad choices, then wanted to put things right. If the gang ever finds him, his life is forfeit, too. Anyone who helps him, helps him at his or her peril.'

'Young man, as noble as you may paint the fellow, that hardly answers my question.'

'Mrs Merridew, Thomas Shepherd's brother's name is James. Mr James Shepherd.'

Now the woman was frowning with the effort of remembering. 'My footman?' she said at last.

'The same. Persuaded by Thomas that the boy's life was in danger, he swore to protect the daguerreotype, but when the gang tracked him to your residence, he too was forced to go into hiding. Under the circumstances, there was only one person he could entrust it to: his Sunday sweetheart—'

Everyone stared as Miss Penelope threw open the library door and ran from the room. Mrs Blake, whose expression showed that she had guessed what was coming, rose and ran after her. Mr Blake, who is not quite as sharp-witted as his wife, pieced the story together a few seconds later and sank down into his chair with a sigh.

'For the edification of Mrs Merridew,' said Mr Betteredge, steadfastly refusing to look in my direction, 'pray continue.'

'Yes, to whom did my footman entrust the portrait?'

'Miss Penelope, miss. She and James were courting.'

'Courting? *Courting*? But that's ridiculous. They never had time to court.'

'They both had Sunday afternoons off, miss.'

Mrs Merridew blinked, as if grappling with a new and disturbing idea. 'Betteredge, do servants court?' she demanded to know.

'It has been known, madam.'

'Oh.' She sat back with a troubled look on her face as she tried to digest this news.

Mr Blake had recovered sufficiently by this point to ask, 'So it was Miss Penelope who slipped the daguerreotype into Aunt Merridew's bag when the gang attacked them in the street?'

'Yes, sir, it was. But she did it with the best of intentions. Surely you can see that?'

'I do, I do. But a boy's life is at stake, Gooseberry. We have an obligation to take this matter to the police.'

'The police, sir?' howled Betteredge. 'But my poor daughter! Her good name will be dragged through the dirt!'

For a second, it looked as if the old man was trying to take a small step forward, but then his body began to crumple.

'Bruff!' cried Mr Blake, springing to his feet. 'Help me!' Supporting the steward by his armpits, the two men assisted him into a chair.

'I'm fine, sir, I'm fine,' complained the old man. 'It was just a slight turn. I shall be as right as rain in a minute or two.'

'What's your opinion, Bruff?' Mr Blake asked in a whisper, as his wife re-entered the room. 'We need to call the police in on this, don't we?'

Mrs Blake froze. 'Franklin, did you not learn a thing,' she asked, '*not a single thing*, from your wretched involvement with the Moonstone? Miss Penelope has told me everything and we are not about to summon the police.'

'But, my dear, we have to do *something*.'

'It occurs to me that we already have one of the finest detectives in London on the case,' she said, turning to me. 'Gooseberry, are you prepared to investigate further?'

'I am, miss.'

'I won't stand for you putting yourself in any danger, mind.'

'No, miss.'

'Mr Blake, of course, will bear all the expenses.'

That was indeed music to my ears. *Per diems* can only get you so far in this life. 'Thank you, miss.'

'There. Then it's all settled.'

Mrs Blake was a most determined woman, I reflected on the journey back to the office. She brooked none of the objections that her wearying husband put forward, often stilling his tongue with a solitary withering look. When she said something was settled, it was settled—much to my own satisfaction, God bless her! But all these admiring thoughts were blown away like thistle seeds in a gale as the cab turned into Gray's Inn Square, for who should come running—*running* no less!—out of Mr Bruff's offices, but the younger of the two Georges. As he bolted into the path of the cab the cabbie had to pull the horse up sharp-ish, sending Mr Bruff and me flying forward in out seats.

'George? What on earth are you playing at?' Mr Bruff screeched out of the window.

'Sir! Sir! I has to call for a copper, sir. There's been a murder…a h'actual murder!'

'*Murder*?'

'Inside, sir,' cried George, pointing.

'Pay the cabbie, Gooseberry,' said Mr Bruff, as he jumped from the carriage to the pavement below and dashed into the building with George.

I paid the man as quickly as I could and then followed them. The door stood open so, as I clambered up the steps, I could see right into the reception area. Every single member of staff had gathered there. They were staring at a figure by the foot of the stairs who was gasping his final breaths. The man's wire-rimmed spectacles sat crookedly across the bridge of his sun-tanned nose, and a dark, red stain blossomed from the breast of his well-cut jacket. It was Mr Treech.

CHAPTER TWELVE

'STEP BACK!' SNAPPED THE diminutive Mr Crabbit, as Mr Bruff pressed his way through the gaggle of clerks. 'I said step back and let your employer through!'

'Mr Crabbit, what in God's name is happening here?'

'This gentleman's been shot, sir.'

'*Here*? On the premises?'

'No, Mr Bruff. He was in this condition when he stumbled in off the street. I fear he's in a bad way. He's been asking for you, sir.'

Mr Bruff knelt by the dying man's side and took hold of his hand. At the sight of his face, Treech rallied a fraction.

'I am not...who you think,' he said, coughing all the while.

'Hush, now,' said Mr Bruff. 'We know. Who shot you, sir?'

'Mallard. Mallard...shot me. The boy...he escaped ...on my watch...overheard...plan to burn the bank down.'

'Who's Mallard?'

'Mallard? All…his idea. Wants…the diamond…' Treech's eyelids began to flutter.

'Stay with me! Stay with me, damn it!'

'Daguerreotype…'

'Yes?'

'The scar…the boy…'

'What about the boy?'

Another fit of coughing. 'I…I picked…the wrong side.' His chest heaved as he attempted a painful, shallow laugh. 'Been…betrayed. Get me…my revenge.'

One last spasm and Treech's body came to rest. Ever so gently, Mr Bruff let go of the man's hand.

'George and George, go and rouse the local police. Mr Crabbit, if you would be so kind as to stay with the body until they get here? Gooseberry, my office, please. The rest of you, back to work.'

Just at that moment, a crumpled ball of paper landed at Mr Bruff's feet. Still kneeling, he picked it up and examined it.

'Who threw this?' he asked, his face turning redder and redder by the second. No one answered.

Standing up, he asked again, 'Who threw this?'

When he still got no reply, he handed the ball of paper to Mr Crabbit.

'Mark my words,' he muttered, as he started up the stairs, 'there will be changes in this office.'

I followed him up. He showed me into his office and shut the door.

'Well, this is a fine kettle of fish! Miss Rachel's wishes be damned, we cannot keep the police out of it now. A murder! And the poor chap dies in my own reception!'

'Sir,' I said, 'with regards to the police, you could always be economical with the truth.' It was a risky thing to suggest, because it could lead him to suspect that this was my own preferred strategy.

'I'm a solicitor, Gooseberry. It's my job to be discreet. The police shall have the bald facts from me and nothing more. But who on earth is Mallard? And what was this diamond he was babbling on about?'

'A mallard's a type of duck, sir,' I said, providing him with a bald fact of my own. As to the question of the diamond, I was sure I knew the answer. For the past year, any mention of a diamond in public had generally meant just one thing: the Kohinoor—the *Mountain of Light*—which had been on display at the Great Exhibition. I had to give Mallard marks for audacity, for the Kohinoor was meant to be the largest diamond in the world.

Mr Bruff sighed. 'So the boy we met at Twickenham has bolted. He could be anywhere by now.'

Effectively scuppering Mallard's well-laid plans, I reflected. At present the man had neither the real maharajah, nor the fake one. The worrying question was whether Mallard shot Treech in a fit of anger over losing the boy, or—more sinisterly—now that his scheme had failed, was he was starting to tie up loose ends?

'Did you catch the fellow's dying confession?' Mr Bruff asked. 'How he picked the wrong side?'

Actually I'd heard every word of it, and I had my own ideas about what it meant. If I was right, then I also knew why Hook had turned on Bertha, and why he now wanted him dead. In a sense it had to do with Pan-faced Dora's mole—the only spot of beauty she ever possessed. Bertha, bless him, didn't know when to keep his trap shut.

'Sir, there's something I wish to follow up,' I said, 'but I'm afraid it will be expensive.'

'How expensive?'

I hadn't a clue how much it cost to have a daguerreotype made, but I knew it cost a lot—and ideally I wanted two of them. 'I'm not sure, sir.'

'I see no problem, since Mr Blake has generously agreed to foot the bill. Have a word with Mr Crabbit when the police are done with him. Tell him you have my blessing.'

It was late in the afternoon when the police eventually departed, having removed the body and taken everyone's statements. Mr Crabbit nearly fell out of his chair when I requested two pounds from him, preferably in shilling coins.

'Don't worry. What I don't use, I'll return,' I promised.

'I shall require receipts,' he reminded me in a trembling voice, quite possibly as a result of handing over the equivalent of half his month's wages from the firm's dwindling reserves.

I found Julius and Bertha working together on money when I got home, but it wasn't going especially well, for they were reduced to using torn scraps of paper instead of actual coins. I was relieved to see that Bertha was still wearing his blue serge suit, for, having forgone dinner due to all the excitement, I was planning to take everyone out for a meal.

Being a Monday evening, the eating house on the Gray's Inn Road—where I normally pick up our supper on my way home—wasn't as packed as it normally was. Mrs Grogan, who runs the place with the help of her husband, was delighted to see I'd brought Julius. She fussed over him and messed with his hair as she showed the three of us to a candle-lit table in the corner.

'So, what's your pleasure to be, gentlemen?' she asked, wiping her hands on her apron.

'Gawd, she thinks I'm an omi,' Bertha grunted in my ear.

'We'll start with soup, if you please, Mrs Grogan, and Julius will have an eel pie. After that, we'll place ourselves in your capable hands and you may serve us with what you judge best. We're all very hungry, you see.' A murder at the office can do that to a person.

The woman beamed at me, then went to fetch our soup.

Halfway through the enormous meal, Bertha burst into tears.

'What's the matter, Bertha?' Julius asked solicitously.

'Nothing, Sprat. Nothing,' he replied, drying his tears with the back of his hand. 'It's just I mustn't let meself get too used to this, that's all. Thank you for this lovely meal, Octopus. I'll never forget these past few days for as long as I live.'

'You certainly won't forget tomorrow.'

'You got something planned, then?'

'Yes, Julius is going to be sick.'

'Am not,' protested Julius. 'I haven't eaten *that* much.'

"Tomorrow you're going to be sick, Julius, *so sick,
you won't be able to go to work.*' The truth is my brother
works hard and without complaint. He deserves a day
off now and again.

'Oh,' he said, as enlightenment came. 'Pity,' he
added, with a serious expression. 'I have to go sick just
when my guvnor was coming round to the idea of
calling me Sprat. Another day might have done it.'

'*Rand,*' Bertha corrected him. 'Comin' *rand* to the
idea.'

I held my tongue.

Tuesday morning dawned bright and chilly. I had
Bertha pack his normal clothes into a canvas bag while
I wrote out a few words on a large sheet of paper, and
then we headed off.

'This ain't some kind of trick to get rid of me?'
laughed Bertha nervously, as he eyed the canvas bag
that contained all his worldly belongings.

'No trick, I promise. This is something you will
love.'

I would have liked us to have taken a cab—for it
would have been the first time Julius had ever ridden
in one—but after the blow-out meal of the previous
evening, I wasn't sure if we could afford it.

'That's where Octopus works,' said Julius, pointing
as we passed Gray's Inn Square.

'That's where *who* works?' I demanded.

'Bertha calls you Octopus. Why can't I?'

'Because you're not Bertha.'

The traffic on Oxford Street was chaotic, as was
the traffic on Regent Street. Carriages and cabs were
banked up all the way to Piccadilly.

'I done that one and that one and that one,' said Bertha, pointing out the shops he'd lifted things from. Since they were all even more select than the stationer's in Bishopsgate, I wondered how he'd managed to charm his way through their doors.

'What do you mean you done them?' asked Julius.

'He just means he's been in them,' I said, purposely glaring at Bertha. 'Look, we're here.'

The three of us stood and stared at the tastefully painted shop-front sign:

Mr William E. Kilburn,
Daguerreotypes of Distinction

A bell rang as I opened the door and a woman appeared from behind a curtain.

'Can I help you?' she asked, eyeing us all with suspicion.

'Good morning, miss. Can you tell me, please, how much does it cost to have a daguerreotype made?'

'It all depends on the size you want.' She gave me a smile as if to say she knew what I was up to, and that she could play this game all day.

'What's the most popular size, miss?' I could play it too.

'A lot of people choose the sixth-plate,' she replied, leaving me entirely in the dark.

'Oh? And how much is a sixth-plate?'

'A sixth-plate? Let me think. A sixth-plate will cost you one pound. Now, are we done here?'

'I'll take two, miss.' Thank God we didn't come by cab.

'You'll take…'

'Two.'

'I…I'll need to take your payment up front.'

'And I,' I said, extracting the bag of shillings from my jacket, 'shall require a receipt when we're finished.'

Having tamed the dragon at the gate, we were led through to the back of the shop, which was lit by an enormous glass skylight. Mr Kilburn was a slightly-built man of about forty-five years of age, with dark, unkempt hair, a full moustache, and a generous sprinkling of freckles.

'Group shot, is it?' he inquired, studying the three of us from what I imagined was an artistic point of view.

'The first one, yes. My friend here will need somewhere to change his clothes.'

'He can change in there,' he said, indicating a small dressing room off a corner of the studio. 'It's quite private.'

As Bertha hurried away to change, I turned to Mr Kilburn and said, 'Would you believe that that was none other than Mr Bertram Gubbins, the Theatre Royal's premier comedic actor, and toast of London society for his role as the drunken butler in last year's production of *"Miss Penelope's Secret"*?'

'Really? He honestly didn't strike me as the type.'

'That's because he's in character, sir. Most actors are content to declaim their parts loudly and accurately, but Gubbins believes in walking around in his character's shoes. For this latest role, he's preparing to play a Covent Garden flower girl.'

'A great big man like that?'

'He is a *comedic* actor, sir,' I pointed out, as Bertha rejoined us, looking utterly relieved to be back in a skirt again. The photographer burst out laughing.

'Very good, sir!' he cried. 'Truly, I applaud you.'

'Wot the 'ell's 'e on about,' growled Bertha, giving him the evil eye.

Hearing the deep bass voice, Mr Kilburn laughed even louder. 'Extraordinary! Absolutely extraordinary! All he needs is a basket!'

'Wot about me damned basket?'

'Oh, how I wish I'd caught his drunken butler! Tell me, sir, why have I never seen you before?'

'Clearly 'cos you ain't bleedin' looked!'

Mr Kilburn doubled up with laughter.

'Look, are we gunna get this duggairiotype done, or are we just gunna stand 'ere all day?'

'No more! No more! I can't take it!'

'Bertha, hush, and let the man do his job.'

Eventually Mr Kilburn calmed down enough to start arranging us in front of the backdrop, a wall of the studio that had been staged to look like a drawing room. He placed Bertha in a chair in the middle, with Julius standing on his left and me on his right. 'You're lucky,' he said, 'it's a nice, clear day. You'll only have to stay still for ten seconds.'

'Ten seconds?' gasped Julius, realizing how impossible that was going to be for him.

'Don't worry,' said Mr Kilburn. 'I'll be bolting you all in.'

Ten minutes later, he'd done just that, bolting us into what he called "*posing frames*".

'Have you ever played at staring matches, to see

who will blink first?' he asked. When nobody nodded their head—because nobody could without ripping away the back of their neck—he said, 'You can still speak, you know.'

'We knows wot starin' matches is, don't we, Sprat?'

'Good. So you're going to have a staring match with me. Ready? On the count of three. One—two—three!'

Still gawping at us with his eyes wide open, he whipped the lens cap off his camera.

'Can I get a copy of that?' asked Bertha, once he'd replaced it again.

'Daguerreotypes aren't Talbotypes, Mr Gubbins. They're one-off originals. You can't print them. But I tell you what. If you'll permit me to take your portrait—at my own expense, of course—and allow me to exhibit it in my celebrity showcase, I'll make another group shot for free, gratis.'

'Wot about a third 'un for me mate, Sprat?'

'You drive a hard bargain, Mr Gubbins. Very well. I believe you're worth it.'

Bertha looked delighted. 'Ready for another starin' match, boys?' he muttered.

Almost an hour had gone by before we got round to taking the daguerreotype I was officially there for. This time it was me on my own, sitting in the chair and holding the piece of paper—with the writing on it—across my chest.

'Son,' said Mr Kilburn, 'I hate to see you wasting your money. Daguerreotypes come out laterally reversed. You'll never be able to read what it says.'

'That's what I'm counting on, sir,' I replied. It

occurred to me, as I sat perfectly still for the fourth time that day, that a dead body would make the perfect photographic subject. It got me thinking again about the double-crossed Mr Treech.

As our portraits needed to be processed and wouldn't be ready till the next day, once Bertha had changed back into his disguise and the dragon had written me my receipt, the three of us set off; Julius and Bertha for our lodgings, and me for the office. Little did I realize as I bounded up the stairs that I was in for quite a surprise.

'Miss Penelope!'

Mrs Blake's maid was seated on the bench outside Mr Bruff's office, while George and George stood shuffling their feet and casting resentful glances in her direction. She looked up when she heard me call out her name.

'Gooseberry, I...'

'Miss, I'm sorry for what I did to you yesterday, but you have to understand I had no choice. Before he knew that you were involved, Mr Bruff was all for going to the police. So I had to tell him, you see, to keep the police out of it, and then he felt obliged to tell the Blakes.'

'I understand, Gooseberry. Really, I do. I suppose I should probably thank you.'

'There's no need to thank me, miss.'

'Gooseberry, is there some place private we can talk? It's important. *Very* important.'

That's the trouble with being an office boy. We had no privacy at all. 'You two!' I snapped. 'Isn't it your dinnertime yet?'

'We's not allowed to go to our chophouse no more,' said the elder George sulkily. 'Mr Bruff's put us both on reducing diets.'

'Yeah, reducing diets.'

Reducing diets or not, I was sure Mr Bruff didn't intend them to starve. 'Why don't you go and get yourselves a hot potato? There's a street vendor on the corner of High Holborn.'

I saw a look cross their faces which suggested to me that they'd never considered this option. They glanced at each other, then bolted for the stairs.

'Now, what can I do for you, miss?'

'This morning I received this.' She opened her small handbag and extracted an envelope. Her face was taut as she handed it to me.

Inside I found a lock of coarse, sandy-blond hair. There was also a note scribbled on a yellowing sheet of paper. It said:

"We got James. If he don't tell us where his brother is, be warned: we'll be coming for you."

CHAPTER THIRTEEN

'GOOSEBERRY, I HAVE NO idea how you can know the things you do, but since you seem to know everything, what can you tell me about this? Who has James? What will they do with him?'

I could hazard a guess on both counts and even speculate on his current whereabouts. Instead, all I said was, 'Miss Penelope, these people are dangerous.'

'James is a good man. If you know anything, anything at all, I beg you to help me.'

I reached in my pocket for a coin. I took it out, looked at it, considered flipping it, then thought better of it. I stowed it away again.

'Miss Penelope, have you told Mrs Blake about this?'

'Not yet.'

'Then I want you to go home and explain it to her. Tell her Gooseberry suggests that she closes Mrs Merridew's residence and has the servants transferred to Montagu Square. She should put them to work on an around-the-clock armed watch. As for yourself, miss, you must not set foot outside the house for the next few days, or at least until you hear from me again. May I keep the note, please?'

'What do you plan to do with it?'

'I'm going to use it to try and get Mr James back for you.'

'So you know where he is?'

'I have a fairly good idea.'

'Will you tell me your plan?'

'I'd rather not, miss.'

She blinked. 'And when do you intend to act?'

'Tonight.'

Retaining the note, I replaced the lock of hair inside the envelope and handed it back to her.

'James is a good man,' she repeated, as she rose and took her leave.

I needed to think, but first I needed to prepare. I headed down to Mr Crabbit's office and handed in my receipt. He was not impressed that I'd managed to spend the entire sum he'd given me.

'*Two* daguerreotypes at a pound a piece? A *pound*! Would one have not sufficed?'

'I sneezed during the first attempt and spoiled it, sir.'

'Costly sneeze! Well, what are you standing there for, boy? I have your receipt; now be about your business.'

'Sir, may I have my *per diem*, please? I've a feeling I'll be needing it tonight.' *If I was lucky enough to survive.*

Mr Crabbit sighed and dug out his petty cash tin. 'Don't think it goes unnoticed what you've been spending this money on,' he warned me. 'Expensive pocket diaries and luxury photographic portraits. And the number of pencils you get through! Here. Seven shillings and sixpence. Now, on no account forget the—'

'The receipts. Yes, sir. Sir?'

'Well?'

'Take a look at this paper, if you please.' I showed him the back of Miss Penelope's note. 'Do we keep anything like this in stock? I just need one or two sheets, so it seems a waste to go out and buy a whole ream of it.' That got him.

'I sincerely doubt you *could* buy such a thing. This paper's yellowed with age. But I may have something here that will serve,' he said, wrestling in the bottom drawer of his desk. God bless misers and hoarders.

'Perfect!' I said, as he handed me exactly two sheets. 'Now, I wonder if I can impose upon you for an envelope, a pen, and a drop of blue-black ink?'

'Would you care to use my desk while you're at it?'

Having worked with the man for six long years, I can recognize his sarcasm when I hear it. 'Not at all, sir,' I replied. 'I can kneel on the cold, hard floor upstairs and use my bench as a desk.' My own particular brand, however, went straight over his head. Not that it mattered; the last thing I wanted was Mr Crabbit peering over my shoulder. I needed privacy for what I was about to do.

Since the day was a Tuesday—a market day—this evening Johnny would be hosting his fights. If Josiah Hook, esquire, remained true to form—as evidenced by the markings in his diary—he would undoubtedly be in attendance. For my plan to work, I had to keep him away from the Bucket of Blood.

Having checked Mr Bruff's office and found it empty (and, yes, I did consider using it for the briefest of moments, but feared Mr Bruff's disapproval if he happened to return), I knelt on the cold, hard floor in front of my bench and opened Miss Penelope's letter. Now, while may I own up to being the slowest, sloppiest lock-pick in all of London, I also happen to be a dab hand at the beautiful and beguiling art of forgery. Whoever had written this note—for, unless a miracle of biblical proportions had occurred, it couldn't have been the illiterate Johnny Knight—they formed their letters slowly and shakily. There was no flow to the penmanship and very few of them were joined up. So far, so good. Next I studied the text.

"We got James. If he don't tell us where his brother is, be warned: we'll be coming for you."

Trying to remember how Johnny spoke, I dipped my pen into the small, brass inkwell Mr Crabbit had loaned me, and wrote:

"Stay clear of the pub. Old Bill's got a raid planned for tonight."

I compared the two notes and decided mine would do nicely. I waited for the ink to dry, then folded it twice and popped it into Crabbit's envelope. Not a minute too soon, for I could hear George and George coming, lumbering up the stairs after their reducing dinner.

'Now, which of you two lads has heard of the

Thames Tunnel?' I asked them, as they eventually appeared at the end the corridor.

'I heard of it,' admitted the elder George. 'It's out Wapping way.'

'Excellent,' I said, handing him the envelope. 'Mr Bruff would like you to deliver this.'

'But I just had me dinner and I ain't had me nap yet…and Wapping's miles and miles away.'

The younger George sniggered.

I extracted a threepenny piece from my pocket. 'You'll need a penny for the entrance fee. Halfway along the tunnel at the bottom of the shaft there's a coffee shop. Look for a gent in his late twenties with a pale complexion and dark hair and a beard. He'll be sitting at a table but, depending on how busy they are, he may or may not be on his own. Approach him and quietly ask if he's the client—quietly, mind. If he says yes, give him the envelope. There's another penny for a piece of cake—'

'Cake?'

'Yes. I can recommend the Dundee cake. It's got lots of lovely almonds on top. You've also got another penny to spend at your discretion.'

'At my what?'

'You can spend it on whatever you like.'

'Cor!'

'And best of all, George, you don't need to worry about bringing back receipts.'

By now the younger George was looking green with envy. 'Why didn't you pick me?' he asked.

'Because you, my friend,' I told him, 'failed to volunteer.'

I had the elder George repeat his instructions back to me until I was sure he knew them by heart. Then I patted him on the shoulder and sent him on his way. Having done all the preparation I could for the time being, I now needed somewhere quiet to think. I took myself outside into the square, and went and sat on one of the benches.

Johnny had taken James, presumably at Mallard's request, to ferret out Thomas's location. Given that the boy I'd met in Twickenham had put paid to Mallard's plans by absconding, that meant there could only be one reason for this. Mallard was desperate to clean house. On the bright side, I couldn't see James giving up his brother—and thank goodness, for it was only that piece of information that was keeping him alive.

Taking James on his own had been a mistake. Johnny should have abducted Miss Penelope, too. Threatened *her* life, not his. But then, Johnny isn't noted for his brains, and nor, I suspect, does he understand what people will do for love. The only person Johnny loves is Johnny.

For quite some time I had been aware of the fact that I would end up having to face Johnny. I'm not trying to excuse my increasingly reckless spending, but if I was about to die—a strong possibility, given that my only advantages over an older, taller, and stronger opponent were my swiftness and brains—I wanted some extraordinary memories, some to take with me and some to leave behind. If the impossible were to happen and James and I made it out alive, it was my sincere hope that Mallard would come to blame Johnny for the loss, and get rid of him, just as he had done with Treech.

A gust of cold wind whipped around the square, lifting piles of leaves into the air and rattling gutters. Shivering, I made my way back inside. George returned shortly before the close of business.

'So what did you spend your penny on, George?' I asked, as he sat down on our corridor bench.

'The monkey,' he answered, though he didn't seem too happy about it. I really should have warned him about the monkey. 'Had to,' he explained after a moment's pause. 'The man I gave the note to asked me a question, and I wasn't going to come all the way back just to ask Mr Bruff. So I asked the monkey instead.'

Oh, God. I hadn't foreseen this. 'What question George?'

'Whether it was still on for tomorrow night.'

'Whether what was on?'

'Dunno.'

'So what did you tell him?'

'I told him I'd go and find out.'

'George, this is important. Did the man see you consulting the monkey?'

'I didn't hurt the monkey!' George protested. 'I wouldn't do that!' He stared at me indignantly.

'Did he see you asking it? Think!'

'Nah. He didn't follow me. He was too busy writing in his little book.'

'And what was the monkey's answer?'

'The monkey? Oh, he said, "*yes*".'

That was fortuitous, since the police raid was entirely

of my own invention, and whatever was planned would most likely go ahead. I reached in my pocket and pulled out a shilling.

'What's this?' George asked, as I placed it in his palm.

'It's to replace the penny you were obliged to use. You can spend it on anything you like, but I hope you'll consider using it to visit the zoo this weekend.'

I don't know if I expected gratitude, but I certainly didn't expect the reaction I got. The coin seemed to puzzle him so much that he couldn't stop frowning at it.

I picked up some eel pies at Mrs Grogan's on the way home. Accompanied by the potatoes that Bertha had cooked, they made a nice enough meal. While Julius got ready to practise his writing, I took Bertha out on to the landing for a quick word.

'Wot's up with you?' he asked. 'You been quiet all evening.'

'Bertha, I have to go out tonight, and I might not be back till tomorrow. I want you to do me a favour. See that Julius gets off to work in the morning, then go and pick up the photographs. If you don't hear from me by tomorrow night, give Julius the picture of me holding the sheet of paper, and pass on this message for me. Tell him I said "*unnecessary*".'

'Unnecessary?'

'He'll know what to do. Listen, Bertha, another thing. I need to borrow your clothes.'

'No problem. I can change out of me disguise in a jiffy.'

'Not your disguise, Bertha. Your normal clothes.

Your skirt, your shawl, your cap and ribbons. I could also do with a knife, if you've got one.'

'Octopus, you're starting to scare me.'

'I'm starting to scare myself. But enough of this. Let's go in before Julius comes looking for us.'

'What word will we do tonight?' asked Julius, as Bertha and I re-entered the room.

I gave my usual reply. 'I don't know…what word would be useful?' All the while, I was studying his eyes. As always, I could see my mother in them.

'How about "*duggairiotype*"?'

I didn't bother correcting him. I knew that if I didn't make it back, he'd soon be speaking permanently like Bertha—the price of having Bertha look after him. A small price, really, when I came to think about it.

'Would you settle for "*picture*"?' I asked. Julius nodded and I wrote out the word.

It was blowing a gale as the cab drew into Long Acre and pulled up by St Martin's Lane. There was hardly any traffic on the roads, yet, despite the cold, the pavements thronged with life. Groups of drunken porters staggered from one pub to the next, while working girls stood warming themselves in front of scalding charcoal braziers, much to the wry bemusement of the roasted chestnut vendors who operated them. With the bag of Bertha's clothes slung over my shoulder, I hopped down from the carriage and had a word with the driver. I knew I could trust him to wait, for he was one of Mr Bruff's regulars and I had ridden up on the box beside him many times before.

I turned the corner and stood for a moment

looking up at the Bucket of Blood, its windows all aglow with a soft, yellow light. Above, dark clouds scudded across the jet-black sky. The door screeched open on its rusty hinges and an elderly couple lurched into the street, taking wild, unsteady steps as they went. I slipped through the door before it closed and, keeping my head down to avoid recognition, made my way quickly across the sawdust-strewn floor.

The fights were held in a yard at the back, with access via a narrow outdoor passage, which customers used as a urinal. Squeezing past a man who was availing himself of the facilities, I arrived at a large flagstoned area that was hemmed in on all sides by neighbouring buildings. Fires blazed in huge tin drums, lighting the central ring, where one man was pummelling another to the ground while onlookers bellowed their support. Behind them, on a raised platform, a good two feet above most people's heads, sat a chair resembling a kind of throne. Johnny's chair, but it was empty. So where the hell was Johnny?

I headed back inside and scanned the room. It was then that I noticed the guard stationed at the bottom of the stairs. I recognized him immediately, even though many years had gone by. It was Colin, who'd been fourteen at the time. Now he was a young man of twenty. I wondered where his twin brother, Eric, was, for the pair had always been inseparable.

'Hello, Colin,' I called out as I approached him.

'My word! If it ain't young Octopus! Where've you been keeping yourself these past six years?'

'Oh, here and there,' I answered, and tapped the side of my nose knowingly. 'Where's Eric?'

Colin gave a sideways nod at the stairs behind him. 'Up there. Johnny just made him his second-in-command.'

'His *deuce*?' That came as a bit of a shock. Eric and Colin had never been especially talented, nor were they natural born leaders. They weren't what I'd consider the violent sort; they were more like a couple of amiable sheep.

'Wait, you ain't come to take his place, 'ave yeh?' He was referring to the fact that I'd once been a deuce myself, a position that even now demanded his loyalty and respect.

'No, Colin, have no fear of that. But I do need to see Johnny.'

'Johnny's a bit tied up at the mo',' said Colin evasively. 'Why don't you come back Thursday?'

'Don't worry,' I said, as I pushed my way past him. 'Johnny will want to see me.'

Colin squirmed as he tried to stop me. It was a half-hearted attempt and he quickly gave up. Throwing him a grin and a quick wink, I padded up the stairs to the corridor at the top.

A door at the end of the hall stood open, giving a narrow view of the spacious room beyond. As I got closer, I spied Eric, Colin's thinner, wirier brother, pacing in circles whilst balancing a gent's cane in his hand. I could see how extremely nervous he was, flinching as he constantly readjusted his grip on the handle. All the while I could hear Johnny screaming at him to put his back into it. Eric set his jaw grimly, raised the cane, and took a few steps back.

'Go on! Get it over with!' cried Johnny, from

somewhere behind him in the room. Eric steeled himself and started running.

I bolted through the doorway, convinced by now that Eric was about to deal James a thrashing. But James wasn't even there. Instead, the object of Eric's wrath was a pane of glass that had been suspended across two high bar stools. As he brought the cane down with all his might, the pane shattered, sending fragments flying into the air. Behind me there came a burst of maniacal laughter. As I turned, I saw Johnny perched on yet another bar stool, well out of reach of the exploding glass.

'Well, well,' he said, as he noticed my arrival. 'If it ain't my old friend, Octopus.'

CHAPTER FOURTEEN

HOW SIX YEARS CAN change a person. The last time I'd seen him, Johnny Knight had been a tall, spotty youth with a mop of wild hair, the unenviable colour of rat's urine. He'd sprung up and out since then, but the greatest difference came in the form of his face. His rotting teeth had caused his cheeks to collapse inwards, puckering his mouth and giving him the appearance of a bitter, old man. I noticed his dress sense hadn't altered any—despite his elevated position—but then, I suppose, neither had mine.

'Heard you was back,' he said, taking a swig from the whiskey bottle he was holding, as two young lads ran forward and began sweeping up the glass. 'Edinburgh, was it?' That's certainly where I told Bertha I'd been. 'As you can see, there's been a few changes round here, so don't go getting any funny ideas. It wouldn't be healthy.'

'It's nice to see you, too, Johnny,' I said brightly.

Johnny frowned, unable to work out whether I was being sarcastic or not. Though "*sarcastic*" may not have been in his vocabulary, he had a keenly honed sense of when someone was being disrespectful to him. *Note to self: do not push your luck.*

'Was that any better, Johnny?' asked Eric, giving me a nod of recognition, albeit a wary one. Like his brother, Colin, perhaps he thought I was here after his job.

'Me old mother could have made a better hash of it,' barked Johnny, 'and she's been dead nigh on ten years. Again! You'll do it again!'

The two lads who'd been clearing up placed another pane of glass across the bar stools. Eric glowered at me and began pacing the room again, attempting to work himself up into a frenzy.

'Remember when you and me were mudlarks together, Octopus?' Johnny turned to me and asked. 'Picking through the stones of the riverbank at low tide? Me, I always got the bits of bone, the scraps of splintered wood. You, you got the copper nails and the lumps of coal. And do you remember when winter came, and we was both stuck on the shore freezing our behinds off? It was me what found us that Ragged School to take shelter in, but even then you had to go one better. You couldn't just accept their hot potatoes and magic lantern shows, and have done with it. No, you had to go and suck up to them teachers with all their bleedin' book learning. You, you had to be clever. But don't think for one minute that you had them fooled. They knew you fell in with the local gang, just like the rest of us. They knew what you got up to when we all went out on a job. Why is it, do you think, that they never grassed us up to the magistrate?'

'Perhaps they were being kind,' I suggested carefully.

Johnny took another swig of whisky. 'Kind? *Kind?* Nah, you got it all wrong. Remember that old coot, what had the whiskers down to here? He took a liking to me. Too much of a liking, if you catch my drift. Swore he'd do anything for me. That's why we was never grassed up. That's why *you* was never grassed up.' Behind me, Eric was raging like a bull. 'Because of that—and *only* because of that—you got to rise up through the ranks. Now—fair's fair—I know that I did too. But it was you what became Ned's second-in-command, not me.'

Johnny paused. He glanced at Eric and, judging him to have reached a sufficiently fevered pitch, screamed the word, '*Now!*' at him at the top of his voice. Sweat pouring from his face, Eric raised the cane above his head and launched himself at the fresh pane of glass.

'What do you call someone who's second-in-command?' asked Johnny, breathing the question into my ear as needles of glass exploded in all directions.

'A deuce?' I whispered back.

'A stooge,' replied Johnny, and he began to howl with laughter. Eric, meanwhile, was swaying as if on the brink of collapse. Johnny sauntered up to him and struck him across the face. 'Again!' he screamed. 'And this time put more backbone in it!'

Bertha was right. Johnny had changed, and not for the better. From what I could see, he'd descended into the depths of madness, and seemed hell-bent on dragging all those around him with him.

'So why are you here?' he asked, as the two lads set

about sweeping up the glass again. 'Come to take Eric's place?' On hearing this, Eric threw me a filthy look. The cane in his hand started twitching.

'I've come to see James Shepherd. I've come to make him talk.'

'*You*?' Johnny's cold, colourless eyes narrowed.

'Our mutual friend sent me. He believes that I may be…well…more persuasive, shall we say, at getting his brother's whereabouts out of him.'

'Oh? And what *mutual friend* would that be?'

'He wouldn't appreciate either of us using his name, now, would he? Let's just call him the Client.'

In the blink of an eye, the whisky bottle was on the floor and Johnny had his hands round my throat. 'Let's not,' he hissed, as he began to squeeze. 'Let's respect him by giving him his proper name.'

'*Hook*,' I gasped, while I could still get the words out. 'Josiah Hook. I work for him.' Johnny didn't relax his grip.

'If that's true you'll know his guvnor's name.'

'Sir Humphrey…Sir Humphrey Mallard.'

Reluctantly Johnny let go of me. I gently fingered the tender muscles of my throat. I'd be wearing the bruises for weeks.

'What makes Joe think you'll get anything out of him? I can be persuasive, yet I got nothing.'

Joe? Clearly Johnny and Hook were as thick as, well, thieves. 'Mr Hook is appreciative of that. But he believes that maybe violence isn't the answer in this particular case.'

'So what you going to do? Ask him *pretty please*? Promise him he'll get to live, if only he gives his brother up?'

'Something along those lines, yes.'

'You're wasting your time!'

'Mr Hook doesn't think so.'

Johnny snarled and bared his sadly diminished set of teeth. He looked set to choke me again.

'Where have you put him?' I asked, shying away from the stench of his mouth. Even the whisky on his breath failed to disguise the smell of decay.

'End of the corridor. Last room on the left. Go knock yourself out.' Then he seemed to have an afterthought. 'Anything you learn,' he added, 'you best report it to me. I get the credit for it, see?'

'Fine by me.'

By this point the lads had replaced the sheet of glass, and Eric had worked himself up into another frenzy. What had happened to the amiable sheep, I wondered? Silly question. He'd come under Johnny's influence. As I closed the door behind me, I heard Johnny shouting, 'Now!'

The room where I found James was icy. Someone had left the window open on purpose and his skin was blue from the cold. First I removed his blindfold. One eye was bloodied and swollen, so swollen that it refused to open; the other blinked in dispirited fear. A hank of shoulder-length hair was missing from above his right ear where someone had taken the shears to it. The stubble I'd seen on his chin on Sunday now had all the makings of a beard.

'I'm going to remove your gag,' I told him, 'but I need you to stay quiet. Do you understand? Nod if you understand me.'

He stared at me with his one good eye, still blinking but otherwise motionless.

'Mr James, my name is Gooseberry. I work for the Blakes, Miss Penelope's employers, and I'm going to try to get you out of here, but you have to promise to do everything I say. Can you nod?' This time there was a slight movement, though I'd scarcely call it a nod. 'Good. Now, no talking, if you please.'

I took Bertha's knife and carefully cut through the kerchief. James spat the small rubber ball out of his mouth that the kerchief had been holding in place.

'I...know you,' he said softly, the words barely making it past his chattering teeth. 'You're the boy... from the zoo. You...threatened to hurt Penelope.'

'Mr James, Miss Penelope is my friend.' This was somewhat of an overstatement, but there was no time to explain further. 'I apologize for the deception, but it was a test to see how you really felt about her.'

'I...love Penelope.'

'I know. But I had to know for certain, so I devised a little test. I'm going to cut you free now, all right? Ready?' In response, James gave another twitch of his head.

I started by cutting through the ropes at his wrists. Whoever tied him up had made a first-rate job of it. There was no way James could have escaped these bonds on his own. I eventually managed to free his hands, then started on the cords that kept him strapped to the chair.

'What did you say your name was?' James asked, as he flexed and stretched his numb fingers. I could feel his body trembling as I hacked away with the knife.

'Gooseberry. At least, that's what they call me at the Blakes'. I actually work for Mr Mathew Bruff, the Blakes' lawyer. A junior clerk at his offices gave me the name.'

'What's your real name?'

'Octavius. Octavius Guy.'

'Why are you helping me, Octavius?'

'Because if I don't, sir, they're going to kill you. You understand that, don't you?'

'But aren't you're risking your life?'

'Yes, Mr James, I am.' I tugged at the ropes and they came away in my hands. James shuddered and stretched his arms. Hugging himself to keep warm, he started rocking back and forth in his chair. 'Sit still now, sir. I'm about to tackle your ankles.'

Though he still kept rubbing himself to get his circulation going, he succeeded in getting his rocking under control. 'Octavius, why are you risking your life for me?' he asked.

'Because Miss Penelope insists you are a good man.'

James nodded, a proper nod this time.

'There,' I said, as I finished the job. James attempted to stand, but his feet refused to bear his weight, and he collapsed back into his chair. I put down the knife and went to help him up. 'Put your arm around my shoulder, sir, and let me take your weight. We'll get you walking again in no time.'

For some few minutes we staggered around the room, until James was able to support himself again. I bent down and opened the canvas bag, and fished out Bertha's clothes.

'Mr James, I need you to put these on. They may

be a little loose on you, but they're going to have to do.'

Suddenly James had his arm around me, pulling me to him. The blade of the knife was pressed against my throat.

'One final question, Octavius…or whatever your name is,' James hissed in my ear. 'Just how would a young lad at a law office—who claims intimate acquaintance with the Blakes—come to know that I was being held here?'

'Mr James, please put the knife down. You're liable to hurt me with it.'

'Answer my question!'

'All right! All right! Six years ago I used to be part of this gang. But then Mr Bruff found me and rehabilitated me. I do know the Blakes, sir, I swear it, *and* I've met Mrs Merridew, in whose household you were once employed.'

'Then tell me something about her, something that that lunatic and his crew wouldn't know.'

'Mrs Merridew?' I had to rack my brains to remember anything about the old lady. Then it came to me. 'She never realized that servants go courting on their afternoons off.'

The blade pressed harder. 'That could be said of all the best families in London!'

'Wait! I have it. When you handed her your notice, she asked if you were quitting on account of the nuisance callers getting on your nerves.'

'And that, my friend, might be nothing more than a lucky guess on your part.'

I could feel the knife's edge digging deeper into

the bruises Johnny had just given me. 'Explosions,' I said quickly. For a moment the pressure abated.

'What about explosions?' asked James.

'She doesn't like them when they occur at night. Gunfire included.'

Slowly James released me. 'I'm sorry about that,' he said. 'I had to be certain that this wasn't some intricate trick to get me to lead you to my brother.'

I held out my hand. 'Knife,' I said bluntly.

'What?'

'Give me my knife back now! Then get into those clothes I brought you, and be quick about it!'

He handed back the knife, then went and examined the articles on the floor.

'Octavius?'

'What?'

'I really am sorry, you know.'

'Then tell me, James, where is your brother, Thomas?'

James's one good eye blinked. 'Honestly, I have no idea. If I need to contact him, I leave a message for him under a bench in Hyde Park. He does the same if he wants to contact me.' He stared at me imploringly. 'That's the truth, I promise. Now do you forgive me?'

'James, just put on the damned skirt.'

While James got changed, I went to deal with Colin, who was still on guard at the foot of the stairs.

'What's up with you?' he asked. 'You look angrier than a poke in the eye.'

Suffice it to say, no acting was required. 'It's Johnny,' I explained. 'He *wasn't* happy to see me. And he's not happy with you for allowing me up there.' The smile on Colin's face faded, and was replaced rather rapidly by a look of alarm. 'If I were you,' I continued, 'I'd make myself scarce for a bit, at least till his temper dies down. Tell him you were dealing with some trouble on the street.'

'Yeah...yeah, of course,' he mumbled, already backing away. 'Trouble on the street...yeah...'

Once he'd turned and fled, I nipped back up the stairs. James had put on Bertha's clothes, and was ready and waiting, the canvas bag they'd arrived in tucked under his arm.

'Keep your head down and keep the shawl pulled tight across your jaw,' I instructed him. 'Move naturally and don't run unless I tell you to, and try not to draw any attention to yourself. I'll be at your side all the way; just follow my lead. I have a cab waiting for us in Long Acre that will take us to Montagu Square. I've asked the Blakes to set up an around-the-clock watch. They'll be armed, so you'll be safe there. Ready?'

'Tell me again,' said James, 'why are you doing this for me?'

'At this point I really couldn't say. Let's just go before I change my mind.'

As we crept along the hallway and down the stairs, I heard one last pane of glass shattering behind the closed door.

It was going on midnight by the time we got to Montagu Square. Despite the lateness of the hour, the whole household rallied to receive Miss Penelope's beau—even Mrs Merridew, who seemed relieved to see her former footman safe, if not quite sound. James was soon divested of Bertha's clothing, then put to bed, so that Cook could treat his wounds. Mrs Blake and Miss Penelope sat on either side of him throughout, pressing him for his story. Mr Blake stood watching from the foot of the bed. I gathered up the clothes, returned them to the bag, and prepared to take my leave. As I reached the hall—where Samuel, armed with his pistol, sat guarding the entrance—I heard the sound of running footsteps following me. I turned and saw both Miss Penelope and Mrs Blake standing there.

'You're not very good at following orders, Gooseberry,' Mrs Blake observed. 'What happened to not putting yourself in any danger?'

'Miss, if you please, I've had a long night and I just want to go home.'

Mrs Blake smiled. 'We are in your debt, young man.'

Miss Penelope came forward and planted a kiss on my forehead. '*I* am in your debt,' she said. 'Thank you for saving James.'

I nodded, and maybe even cracked a smile myself. Samuel opened the door for me and let me out, and I jogged down the steps to the waiting cab.

The room was in darkness when I got to my lodgings. I could hear Julius's slumbering tones over by the stove.

'You all right, Octopus?' came a soft voice out of the dark.

'Yes, Bertha. I'm all right.'

'You done wot you was gunna do?'

'Uh-huh.'

'Are we safe?'

'It would be best if you kept wearing your disguise,' I replied.

'Wot about you, Octopus?'

'What do you mean?'

'I'm just saying, will you need a disguise now?' When I didn't answer, he said, 'I put your bed-roll out for yeh, just in case. Come and get some shut-eye. You'll be tired.'

I woke up late on Wednesday morning. Julius and Bertha were long gone: Julius to the fish stall and Bertha to pick up the daguerreotypes. I went and ate a leisurely breakfast at Mrs Grogan's, then made my way to work. Feeling the need to replenish my sadly diminished funds, my first port of call was Mr Crabbit. Needless to say, he was furious at my lack of receipts— so furious that he insisted on sending for Mr Bruff. Thankfully, Mr Bruff had already received a note from Mr Blake, lauding my actions of the previous evening. Mr Bruff, bless him, politely but forcefully reminded Mr Crabbit that he had given me his word that receipts for my *per diems* would not be required.

The slightly warmer, overcast afternoon saw me standing on Leadenhall Street, gazing up at East India House. How was I ever going to get inside, I wondered—not just through its portico entrance, you understand—but *inside the company*, with access to Sir Humphrey Mallard and his cronies? And, just supposing that somehow I did manage this, how was I ever going to bring them to book for what they'd done? My mind, I'm sorry to say, was a blank. Even as I let out an audible sigh, fate lent a hand—a hand that literally grabbed me by the shoulder.

CHAPTER FIFTEEN

I CANNOT DENY THAT I nearly jumped out of my skin as I felt the hand land on my shoulder. My first instinct was to bolt, but I was prevented from doing so by a second that seized me firmly by the collar. For the pickpocket, one reason to sport an overly-large jacket is so you'll have room to stow the things that you filch; another is that it's easy to shrug off if someone makes a grab for the collar. My assailant must have known this, for he went directly for my shirt.

'Calm down, boy,' hissed a voice in my ear. 'You're making a spectacle of yourself, and I dare say you wish to avoid making public displays…especially here, in front of East India House.'

The voice trembled with a deep undertone of melancholy, so doleful that the speaker might well have been ruminating on mankind's fall from paradise, rather than giving me a warning. This sonorous quality struck a chord in my memory, and I raised my head and looked.

'Sergeant Cuff!'

'Gooseberry.' Steely light-grey eyes stared down at me from a yellow, weather-beaten face. They twinkled as my old acquaintance slowly relaxed his grip.

Before his retirement to the small town of Dorking, Sergeant Cuff had been Scotland Yard's most celebrated detective. Three years earlier, I'd had the privilege of working with him to uncover the truth behind the Moonstone gem. The last time I'd seen him, he'd been dressed in whites and greys, and looked every bit the country gent that he's not. The man who stood before me now wore clothes of sombre black, with a single flourish of white at his throat in the form of a natty cravat. Being so lean and wiry, he had the air of a seasoned undertaker, and one who might do rather well for himself in such a career.

'I thought you retired to grow roses, Sergeant Cuff.'

'I did, lad, I did. But it would seem that *you* haven't…'

'I'm sorry?'

'Retired, boy. This is the third time I've seen you here this week.' When I put on my *puzzled face*, he tutted and proceeded to tell me, 'You were here on Thursday, you were here on Saturday, and you're here again today. I ask myself, could it be that you've found yourself employment in these hallowed halls, *or…*'

'Or what, sergeant?'

'Or do you happen to be working on a new case, Gooseberry?'

He smiled at me gravely, drat him.

It's one thing to run rings around the upper class, who can barely see past the tips of their noses. It's quite another to go head to head with the good Sergeant

Cuff. Retirement aside, he was essentially a working-class man who had kept company with—and also arrested—the most talented crooks and thieves in the land. He'd learned a trick or two in his time. He was not someone, like Mr Bruff, who would be dazzled by the merest smokescreen; he was a much tougher wheel of cheese. Sergeant Cuff could read men's hearts.

'It's a long story,' I replied.

'Excellent. I love a good story, and I have a feeling I shall wish to hear it all.' He emphasized the word "*all*". 'There's a public house down that alley there that serves a mighty fine porter,' he continued. 'We shall retire to its gloomy interior for refreshments and you can tell me everything.' You can guess for yourself which word he emphasized this time.

By common consent we chose a window seat, so that we could actually see what we were drinking. Sergeant Cuff had his glass of oily, brown bitter in front of him. I had my bottle of ginger beer. I started by explaining about the portrait: who it depicted, how it was found, and who put it there. At some point the sergeant pursed his lips and muttered, 'The Maharajah of Lahore, you say? Hmmm. Significant. Undoubtedly significant.'

If he considered that significant, I don't know how he'd have rated my next revelation, but beer sprayed from his lips in all directions when I told him about our trip to Cole Park Grange.

'How did you know the boy you saw was an impostor?' he demanded.

'Besides his remarkable ability to pick pockets? Well, the note specifically said that the maharajah would be put to death; it didn't say, "*I'll* be put to death".'

'Good point.' Sergeant Cuff was looking seriously worried. 'But this can only mean…' His voice trailed off as he lifted his glass to his lips.

'That they were planning to use the boy to steal the Kohinoor diamond,' I said, finishing his sentence for him. Beer went spraying everywhere again. I discreetly took out my handkerchief and gave my face a wipe.

'Gooseberry, you really will have to explain yourself. How on earth do you arrive at that conclusion?'

I told the sergeant about how Mr Bruff had claimed to have deposited the daguerreotype with his bank and how the bank was subsequently razed to the ground; how the Indian lad I'd met had absconded and how, as a consequence, Mr Treech had been shot. I recounted the man's dying words as fully and accurately as I could.

'As soon as he mentioned the word "*diamond*",' I explained, 'I immediately thought of the Kohinoor. It stands to reason that whatever these people were after had to be worth the expense and the trouble of getting it. What better to fit the bill than the largest diamond in the world? Of course, now that the boy they had posing as the maharajah is on the run, their plans are naught but ashes.'

Sergeant Cuff nodded thoughtfully. 'Hold on,' he said. 'You say this chap Treech was shot on Monday. Yet I saw you coming out of the East India Company, looking rather pleased with yourself, last Saturday— two days before the man's dying confession.'

I told you the sergeant was sharp. I began to explain

Johnny Knight's role in the matter and how he reported to a man named Josiah Hook. I was careful not to give away how I had come by Hook's name for, as far as I'm aware, the sergeant is still ignorant of my skills, and I should like to keep it that way. I described how I'd followed Hook back to Leadenhall Street, and my little ruse with the diaries to establish not just where he worked, but for whom he worked: Sir Humphrey Mallard.

'Mallard, eh?' The sergeant's face looked grim as he pondered the name. 'So what did they do with the real maharajah, I wonder?'

'He's safe for now,' I assured him, and went on to explain about James's wayward brother, Thomas, and how he'd had a change of heart and taken the maharajah and his guardian into hiding.

'Do you know,' said the sergeant, 'I once made a prediction about you, lad, to Mr Franklin Blake himself. I said that one day you would do great things in my late profession. It seems you have proved me right.'

'Your *late* profession, sir?' Sergeant Cuff was not the only person at the table with brains enough to see through smokescreens.

His eyes narrowed. 'You heard me, lad. My *late* profession.'

'So it's just a coincidence that you happened to be standing outside the East India Company on the occasion of every one of my visits?' The great man's face remained impassive. With control like that, he could have done great things in *my* late profession. 'If I recall rightly, sir, you were all too keen to retire and grow your roses. The only reason you returned to the

Moonstone case was the debt you felt to Mrs Blake's mother, who you considered had overpaid you for your time.'

The sergeant gave a guarded nod. 'There were professional reasons, too,' he added. 'I don't like being wrong. I don't like unresolved cases. I prefer my world to be orderly.'

'So I find myself wondering,' I pressed on, 'what it would take to bring you out of retirement once again? Another unpaid debt, perhaps, but not necessarily of a financial nature? The threat to a loved one? A sense of obligation or duty?' I was studying his eyes as I ran through my list. His eyelids flickered ever so slightly at the suggestion of obligation and duty.

'A sense of obligation or duty, then,' I surmised. 'But to whom? To someone of great importance, I would wager. Maybe even the highest in the land… Her Majesty Queen Victoria herself, perhaps? No— not the Queen.' His eyelashes had wavered, but not in the way I was expecting. 'The Prime Minister, Lord John Russell, then? No? Then there's only one person it can be.'

'Really?'

'The Queen's husband, Prince Albert.'

Sergeant Cuff puckered his lips and gave a long, low whistle. 'I take my hat off to you, young detective. I couldn't have done better myself. In fact, it's fair to say that you have surpassed me in every way.'

'Surpassed you, sir?'

'While I've been keeping my eye on the building at the Prince's request, you've been unearthing the plot that I should have had wind of from the start.'

'But I had the good fortune of being called for by the Blakes when Mrs Blake's aunt discovered the daguerreotype. It was just a stroke of luck, sir.'

'Tell me again about the boy, this impostor of Mallard's. You're certain he's on the run?'

'As certain as I can be, sir. The boy didn't seem to be a willing accomplice.'

'Good. All the same, it wouldn't do to become complacent. I imagine they're searching for him as we speak.' It was a possibility, of course, though after seeing Johnny and Eric's performance the previous evening, it seemed unlikely. Johnny was too caught up in his own madness to organize anything as structured as a search. 'But what if they *were* able to find him in time?' the sergeant added, posing the question to himself.

'In time for what, sir?'

'The reception they're holding tonight at East India House.'

'Reception?' Something stirred at the back of my mind. Something that James had told Miss Penelope when he met her at the zoo: how Thomas believed they only needed the maharajah out of way until the day after the reception. 'What's this reception in aid of, sir?'

Sergeant Cuff laughed. 'Do you mean to tell me that there's something you *don't* know?'

'Please, sir. I've a feeling it may be important.'

Instead of answering me directly, the sergeant posed a question of his own: 'Are you aware of the Kohinoor diamond's history? Its recent history, I mean.' He gave me a reproving look as I shook my head, as if to say that I should have made it my business to find out. 'Until a couple of years ago it belonged to Duleep Singh.'

'So that's how the young maharajah comes into it?'

The sergeant nodded. 'Yes, lad. He inherited it from his father, Ranjit Singh, who obtained it from a man named Shujah Shah Durrani, the deposed ruler of Afghanistan, as the price for granting Durrani asylum in Lahore. When East India Company troops won the Second Anglo-Sikh War and annexed the Punjab, the stone was counted among the spoils and, as such, its ownership transferred to Queen Victoria. Last year it went on display at the Great Exhibition in Hyde Park. Did you happen to see it there?'

'No.' Not at a shilling a pop, I didn't. That was in the days before my *per diem*.

'Being the largest diamond in the world, it naturally drew in the crowds, but it also caused quite a controversy.'

'In what respect, sir?'

'It didn't catch the light, lad. No matter how they angled it in its glass display case, it simply didn't sparkle the way that everyone imagined it ought to. The powers-that-be decided that something needed to be done about it. So the stone is to be re-cut, and Prince Albert himself is to oversee the operation personally. At tonight's reception, he'll be handing the gem over to the firm that has been tasked with doing the work.'

'And the Maharajah of Lahore was expected to attend?'

'Yes, as a guest of honour. Gooseberry, are you all right?'

No, I wasn't all right. I had a bad feeling about this.

Some phrase, some turn of words the sergeant had used had triggered a sense of foreboding but, for the life of me, I couldn't think what.

'Sir, there'll be adequate security precautions taken tonight, won't there?'

'I am in charge of all the arrangements,' Sergeant Cuff replied warily.

'And I take it Prince Albert isn't bringing the diamond himself?'

'No, that would be highly irregular.' The sergeant leaned across the table, tapped the side of his nose with his forefinger, and addressed me in a whisper. 'Officially it will be transported by an armed escort, due to arrive at six this evening. Unofficially two of my best men will be bringing it by a different route. The reception, which starts at eight, is to be held in the banqueting hall and my men will stay with it throughout. It's a large room, so I've arranged for twelve of my officers to pose as waiting staff. They'll be able to circulate while keeping their eyes peeled for any sign of trouble.'

'Sir?'

'Yes, Gooseberry?'

'Can I…*may* I…please attend? I have a very bad feeling about tonight.'

The sergeant looked at me and smiled. 'I thought you'd never ask,' he replied. 'Come on. Let's go see if we can't get you kitted out. I expect they'll have livery in your size. You won't be able to wear that bowler hat of yours, mind, and I imagine we'll have to hide those bruises round your throat.'

By a quarter to eight I was garbed up like the rest

of the waiters—Sergeant Cuff's men included—in white shirt and breeches, and a tail coat of red and gold brocade. We were receiving our final orders from the steward, which included strict instructions on how we were to act—and *not* act—should we be lucky enough to encounter His Royal Highness the Prince. It all seemed like a great fuss about nothing, if you ask me. I mean, who amongst us would ever consider trying to shake the man's hand?

'To your trays!' barked the steward. 'Quickly now!'

I picked up a large silver platter of puff pastry cases filled with some grey-looking sludge. As I lined up in the queue for the banqueting hall, I tested one by pushing the parsley garnish aside and dipping my finger in it. I think it was a concoction of chicken livers—it was hard to tell—perhaps with some sherry thrown in. The sherry saved it. Still, it wasn't up to Mrs Grogan's standards, and I began to feel sorry for the prince.

'And out you go!' the steward commanded. 'No jostling, now! Proceed in a stately, dignified manner!'

The banqueting hall was lit entirely by candles, their beams caught and reflected in the crystals that drooped like shimmering fruit from the chandeliers. A fire blazed in an ornate fireplace that was large enough to accommodate an ox roasting on a spit. There was even an orchestra of sorts, made up entirely of string players, whose main aim in life seemed to be to play as quietly and inoffensively as possible. Small groups of people stood chatting together, their glasses charged to the brim by the circling wine waiters. I myself began to circle, but nobody seemed to fancy the savouries on my tray.

I spied Sergeant Cuff by one of the windows, keeping a wary eye out. I would have gone over and joined him, but just at that moment some chap at the door announced the imminent arrival of the prince:

'Ladies and gentlemen, I present His Royal Highness Prince Albert of Saxe-Coburg and Gotha, Duke of Saxony.'

The waiters had been warned to move to the sides of the hall, stand stock still, and pretend to be invisible. With a stately, dignified gait that the steward would have been proud of, I made my way over to the orchestra stage, and stood like a marble statue as the prince made his grand entrance. I decided to chance a sneaky glance at the doorway, but my eyes never quite made it that far.

As the guests started bowing and curtseying, the only people left upright were the waiting staff. In the opposite corner of the room, staring at me with a furious expression on his face, stood Johnny Knight, togged up in a wine waiter's outfit. And next to him, in similar attire, stood Eric.

Suddenly I knew the phrase that had bothered me when Sergeant Cuff was talking about the diamond: "*no matter how they angled it in its glass display case*". Its *glass* display case. Dear Lord, Johnny Knight may not have been as mad as he appeared after all.

CHAPTER SIXTEEN

THE ORCHESTRA, WIELDING THEIR instruments loudly for once, struck up a fanfare—no easy task for a bunch of string players without a horn in sight—as the prince and his escort of three grave-looking gentlemen entered the banqueting hall. Prince Albert surveyed the room with a somewhat bewildered expression, as if he couldn't quite understand why all the guests were bowing to him or—perhaps—why all the waiters were not. He was a pale-skinned gentleman with light blue eyes and a mop of dark hair that had long since receded, leaving him with a high forehead. He sported a fine pair of sideburns all the way to his jaw line, which, together with the receding hair, created an almost perfectly oval frame for his face. It gave the impression that, instead of showing any actual flesh, he was wearing a porcelain mask.

Slowly the guests began to rise, only to replace their former bowing with a round of muted clapping. If anything, His Royal Highness looked even more uncomfortable with this. Turning to the most senior of his men, he whispered something in his ear. The man raised his hand and gestured to the orchestra, who quickly struck up a waltz. It was barely audible.

People were starting to circulate again. I looked to see where Johnny and Eric had got to, but they'd both vanished. I did spot Josiah Hook, however, dressed to the nines and looking every bit the kind of young gentleman who'd add the term *esquire* to his name. I began to make my way across the room to warn Sergeant Cuff, but was stopped in my tracks as Colin appeared before me, also kitted out as a wine waiter. He looked none too pleased to see me. Within seconds he was joined by two others, effectively hemming me in by the side of the stage. I would have tried catching the sergeant's eye, but by now he too had disappeared.

'You got me into so much trouble,' snorted Colin, whose jaw appeared to have taken a recent battering.

'Yes, sorry about that,' I replied, then added, 'but it looks like you have more trouble coming your way,' as I noticed the prince's party rapidly approaching.

Colin threw them a glance, but stayed where he was.

People were bowing and moving aside as Prince Albert headed towards the stage. He stopped a few feet away from me and regarded the orchestra thoughtfully. He opened his mouth and asked a question, which sounded like, '*Ken the note ply lot earthen this*?' The musicians glanced nervously at each other.

'You heard His Royal Highness,' said the senior dignitary at his side. 'Louder!'

The musicians played louder. '*March bitter*,' remarked the prince. '*And water these find a liquor sea spray*?' he asked, turning to me. I gaped up at him, blinking.

'Look, the boy's clearly in awe of you, Your Highness,' the dignitary responded, and everybody laughed.

Though not in awe exactly, I *was* however speechless, having no idea just what was being asked of me. I wasn't even sure if the prince was speaking English. Colin and his cronies took this opportunity to melt into the crowd, positioning themselves where they could pounce on me again, and in a hurry, should the need arise.

'*The look entry king*,' mumbled the prince, reaching for the very pastry I'd had my finger in scarcely ten minutes before. I quickly spun the tray around so that he'd pick a different one. 'Tell me,' he said, examining the pastry I was offering him, '*water the cold*?' His hand paused in mid-air.

'What are they called, boy?'

'*Oh*! Pastries?' I suggested. 'Savouries? I think they're made with chicken livers, sir, but it's very hard to tell.'

'Your Royal Highness,' said the dignitary, addressing himself to me.

'What?'

'"I think they're made with chicken livers, *Your Royal Highness*".'

I studied the man's puffy, red face, wondering if by any chance he was related to Mr Bruff. 'Oh…sorry, yes, of course,' I said at last. 'I think they're made with chicken livers, Your Royal Highness, but it's very hard to tell. They're not as good as Mrs Grogan's, see.'

'Whose?' asked the prince, settling again on the one I'd had my finger in.

'Mrs Grogan's. She runs the best eating house on the Gray's Inn Road, Your Royal Highness. You should think about going there sometime.' I gave my tray another spin, but to no avail, for this time he'd kept his eye trained on the pastry in question. 'Here, why not try this one?' I picked up choicest of the batch and held it in front of his face.

'I think the lad's a little simple,' the senior dignitary whispered in the prince's ear, just as the prince snatched the one he'd been after all along.

He stuffed it in his mouth and chewed on it appraisingly, nodding several times before he gave his judgement: '*You contest dash hairy.*'

The dignitary selected one and took a bite. 'You certainly can, Your Highness,' he said, seemingly agreeing with him.

'*The sack white nice,*' said the prince, taking another, though not the one I had in my hand. 'Hmmm...*note bed atoll. Half the let for low me.*'

'Stay at His Highness's side, boy; he may require more. And no more small talk, understand?'

'Understood, sir.'

The prince set off towards the middle of the room. I followed, platter in hand, walking with the stately, dignified gait that I now had down pat. All the guests bowed before him as we moved through the crowd, and I began to get a sense of what life was like for him. He was a ship ploughing a sea of bodies in constant motion. I began to feel seasick. As he came to a halt under the central chandelier, I noticed everyone staring at him and talking. Any fool could tell that that they were talking about him. No wonder he seemed embarrassed by it all.

'Chin up, Your Royal Highness,' I whispered to him softly, so that the senior dignitary couldn't hear. 'They can't *all* be talking about you.' The prince looked down at me and smiled. 'Here, have another pastry,' I suggested. I held up my platter but, just as I did, a hand thrust a bottle under his nose.

'More wine, Your Imperious Majesty?' It was Colin, who was glowering at me even as he spoke. In fact, he was so intent on intimidating me that he failed to notice the silence that was overtaking the room. It was only when the orchestra stopped playing that he finally looked about, and saw that everyone was staring at him rather than the prince.

'Imbecile!' snapped the dignitary. 'That is *not* a proper form of address for His Royal Highness! Guards! Remove this oaf at once!'

'No!' begged Colin, looking at the man with pleading eyes. 'I'm needed here—I'm really needed here!'

'You most definitely are *not* needed here,' came the reply. Two guards from the door appeared and bundled the bewildered Colin from the hall. The dignitary mopped his brow, then turned to the prince and said, 'Your Highness, I cannot apologize enough.'

The prince nodded and said, '*Lettuce half music.*'

The dignitary lifted his hand and signalled to the orchestra, who quickly struck up another waltz.

'What did he do wrong?' I whispered in the prince's ear.

'Apart from implying that I'm overbearing? He addressed me as one would a king,' the prince whispered back, enunciating every word perfectly, 'yet I can never be king. A minor embarrassment for me, but major embarrassment for everyone who heard him draw attention to the fact, no? Son, your eyes are bulging.'

'You speak English!'

'Naturally I do! Just promise not to tell anyone. Heaven forbid! People might come to expect conversation from me, and what would I have to talk about?'

All through this hushed exchange, the dignitary—a florid, portly man who gave the prince a run for his money in the whiskers department—was getting redder and redder in the face. I think nothing would have pleased him more than to have me removed from the hall, too.

'Your Highness,' he said at last, interrupting us to stem his imminent apoplexy.

'Yes? *Wet a sit?*'

'It's time to present the diamond, sir.'

'*Egg salad!*' Prince Albert turned to me and murmured, 'And about time, too.'

The senior dignitary and the elder of the other two men walked slowly towards the back of the hall. The crowd parted before them, opening up a splendid view, for both myself and the prince, of a small mahogany table set against the far wall. Just as they reached it, two stewards came shuffling in, bearing a velvet-draped, rectangular object between them. This they positioned on the table top with painstaking care, fussing over the folds of the cloth for what seemed like minutes and minutes. Finally they turned to the dignitary and nodded.

'Your Royal Highness, ladies and gentlemen,' he announced, 'I present to you the Kohinoor diamond!'

The crowd gasped as the two stewards whipped away the cover, revealing a glass case containing a large, dark, amber-coloured stone.

'Did you see it on display at the Crystal Palace?' whispered the prince.

'No, Your Royal Highness. I couldn't afford the admission.'

'"*Sir*" will suffice, lad. Let us address each other as gentlemen. What is your name?'

'Octavius, sir, though most people call me Gooseberry.'

'Would you like to see the Kohinoor, Octavius? Yes? Then follow me.'

With both of us walking at a slow, stately pace, we set off down the broad walkway left by the retreating guests. Now the people on either side of us dipped rather than bowed, due to the cramped conditions they found themselves in. I scanned the crowd, but though I spied a number of waiters and wine waiters— Sergeant Cuff's men included—I saw no sign of Johnny and Eric.

The closer we got to the diamond, the more detail became apparent. The stone was enormous, the size and shape of a baby tortoise shell. It had been cut to resemble one, too. You'll forgive me for being fanciful when I say that it bore a suggestion of *trapped smoke*. It looked nothing like any of the diamonds I'd handled during my time in the Life—nor those that I'd seen after, for that matter, adorning the fingers, earlobes, and throats of Mr Bruff's female clients.

The prince and I were barely ten paces away from the cabinet when it happened. From the left side of the hall, Eric came charging at the case like a raging bull. At precisely the same moment, Johnny's wine waiters struck, pushing anyone and everyone near them to the ground. Knowing that glass was about to go flying, I ducked in front of the prince, threw myself at him, and screamed, 'Down!'

As the prince toppled backwards, shards of glass rained down on top of us, missing his face, but catching me in the back of the neck. Amidst the screams and the sobbing, I heard Eric's roar of triumph bellowing out through the hall.

Suddenly I felt hands grab me, wrenching me off the prince and spinning me round. I looked up at my captor and recognized him at once as one of Sergeant Cuff's men.

Whether or not he recognized me in turn, he didn't relax his grip. 'Attack His Royal Highness, would you?' he growled.

'No, you got it wrong! I was only trying to protect the prince! I too am with Sergeant Cuff!'

'I got him!' boomed a voice, drowning out my protests, so loud that everybody in the hall froze on the spot. Standing amidst the shattered glass, Johnny was clutching a kneeling Eric by the roots of his hair. Eric looked shocked, betrayed, and every bit as baffled as I myself was. Johnny, who was clearly delighting in being the centre of attention, bawled, 'I got the thief!' again, then reached into Eric's pocket and drew out the diamond, holding it up for everyone to see. Sergeant Cuff, who was only a few feet away, came forward and took it from his hand. He examined it momentarily, turning it over and peering at the surface.

Order was beginning to be restored throughout

the room. Two guards appeared and took charge of Eric. When I tried calling out that they should be taking Johnny too, the man who had me clapped his hand across my mouth to gag me. Transformed once more into an amiable sheep, Eric allowed himself to be led away without protest. The same could not be said of Johnny's other men, who were fighting tooth and nail as they were dragged from the hall. When my captor started prodding me towards the doors, I realized that I was to be included among them.

'Sergeant Cuff!' I screamed through his fingers, while I wrestled like an eel in his grip. 'Sergeant Cuff! Help!'

Hearing my muffled pleas, the sergeant looked up. 'You can give that one into my charge, Evans,' he said, raising an eyebrow at me. 'I doubt he'll try to run away.'

'But, sir, he attacked His Royal Highness.'

The prince was looking shaken, but at least he was on his feet again. '*Heated nose arch thing*,' he told the man sternly, and then turning to me, as clear as a bell, he added, 'Thank you, Octavius. You literally saved my skin.'

The senior dignitary, who'd been stationed close enough to the exploding glass to have received a number of minor wounds, approached the sergeant and spoke quietly to him for a moment. In all the kafuffle, Johnny had vanished. I spotted Eric's brother Colin, though. Having managed to sneak back into the hall, he was standing by the doors with a look of utter shock on his face.

The sergeant summoned Evans, the man who'd

dragged me off the prince, and handed the florid, portly dignitary the gem. I went and joined Sergeant Cuff as the two men moved away, taking the diamond with them.

'Sir, that man who apprehended the wine waiter was none other than Johnny Knight, the head of the gang I was telling you about.' The sergeant regarded me gravely. 'He *planned* this, sir, so it makes no sense at all that he would actively participate in his own man's capture…unless—' In my mind's eye I could see Johnny murmuring a question in my ear: what do you call someone who's second-in-command? When I'd suggested the term *deuce*, he'd laughed and told me, '*Stooge.*'

'Unless?' prompted the sergeant.

'Unless he substituted the diamond for a replica.' The words just fell out of my mouth. 'Then, hero of the day, he's free to disappear.' Just as I'd told Mrs Blake at the start of this case, of the two ways of lifting things, the second is infinitely more satisfying. *While the gang is wreaking chaos and everyone's attention is diverted, somebody else—someone on the spot who seems quite unconnected with any of the troublemakers—he stealthily slips the desired items inside his jacket. Once the gang has scarpered, that person calmly walks away, taking his booty with him.*

'But he made no such substitution,' said the sergeant, breaking my train of thought.

'What?'

'I guarantee you he handed me the Kohinoor itself. The diamond was no replica.'

'How can you be sure?'

Sergeant Cuff blushed. 'Fearing just such a situation,

I took measures.'

'Measures?'

'I *did* something to it, if you must know.'

'*Did* something?'

'Gooseberry, does it really matter what?'

I put on my *hurt face* and blinked a bit. 'I suppose not,' I sniffed. Bertha would have been proud of my performance.

'If you must know,' said the sergeant, 'I took a roll of brown paper tape and tore off a tiny piece of it. Then I licked the gummed edge and affixed it to the underside of the gemstone. You couldn't really see it unless you looked for it. When this Johnny character handed me the diamond, it was the first thing I checked. It was exactly where I put it.'

'Genius!' I cried. I meant it, too. I really couldn't have done better myself. Unfortunately it brought us back to square one, though, for Johnny's actions no longer made any sense. Could it be that, in the heat of the moment, he'd *forgotten* to switch the diamond? Or was he just as mad and deluded as I'd originally thought? I pictured the look that I'd seen on his face, the look of someone who's just succeeded in bringing off a major coup. No, I was missing something here. 'Where is the diamond now, sir?'

'With Sir Humphrey Mallard.'

'*What?*'

'With Sir Humphrey Mallard,' repeated the sergeant.

'The man you gave it to? That florid, portly gent?' To my horror, I saw the sergeant nodding. 'But he's the one behind all this! Why did you give it to *him?*'

'I had no choice. As the person who negotiated

the Kohinoor as part of Britain's settlement after the Anglo-Sikh War, it's his task to hand it over to the head of the firm charged with re-cutting the stone. Given this evening's events, the transaction's now to be held in private. Don't worry…the diamond is safe. Evans will have his eye on it. Gooseberry, what's the matter?'

I barely heard Sergeant Cuff, for I was deep in thought. *Somebody else—someone on the spot who seems quite unconnected with any of the troublemakers—he stealthily slips the desired items inside his jacket.* Not Johnny, but rather the senior dignitary in charge: Sir Humphrey Mallard.

'If everything had gone strictly to plan tonight, would Mallard have had a chance to touch the gem?'

The sergeant frowned. 'No, he wouldn't. His role was purely ceremonial.'

'Johnny didn't make the exchange, sir, because Mallard's going to do it. It was Johnny's job to make sure that he could…and to provide a plausible scapegoat in the form of Eric for when the replica is found to be a fake.'

'If you're right,' said the sergeant, 'then we have no time to lose.'

'No…no, sir,' I warned him. 'Timing is everything now. Until Mallard exchanges the diamond, there is nothing we can prove. You said this transaction was taking place in private?'

'Follow me,' said the sergeant, setting off at a rapid pace, and summoning one after another of his men along the way. Some he tasked with searching the building for Johnny. Others he sent off—at my suggestion—to investigate the Bucket of Blood. The rest of them trailed behind us to a suite at the back of the building. The chamber's four occupants looked up in surprise as the sergeant and I burst into the room.

Mallard, who was on the point of placing the diamond in a plush-lined casket, froze. His counterpart, whom I recognized from earlier, frowned. Evans, the sole person standing, glanced over at the sergeant with a questioning look. Only the prince spoke.

'Octavius! Sergeant Cuff! Is there a problem here?'

'No, Your Highness,' replied the sergeant. 'I'm sure everything's perfectly in order. Sir Humphrey, won't you continue?'

The portly man's hand was trembling as he lowered the gem into the box. His face was flushed. Reluctantly he closed the lid. As he held out the casket, I saw a bead of sweat working its way down his cheek.

But still he seemed unwilling to relinquish it. The man sitting opposite him had to pull it out of his hands.

Had he failed to switch the diamond and didn't want to give the real thing away? Or did he know the game was up and was reluctant to hand the replica over while there was still a chance to switch it back?

'Sir Humphrey, I require you to stand,' said the sergeant.

Quaking, the man rose to his feet. I applied my pickpocket's eye to his generously-cut apparel.

'The inside left breast pocket of his waistcoat,' I whispered in the sergeant's ear.

The sergeant deftly inserted his hand and pulled out a smoky-brown diamond. I held my breath as he turned it over.

There, on the back, was glued a tiny strip of brown paper tape.

CHAPTER SEVENTEEN

THOUGH WE HAD MALLARD in custody, Josiah Hook—his underling—slipped the net and escaped. We could only surmise that he'd seen Sergeant Cuff rallying his men, realized what was about to go down, and immediately took flight. We had more pressing matters to deal with, however, for word arrived from the Bucket of Blood: Johnny was holed up in one of the upstairs rooms, firing his pistol at anyone who tried to enter. So far two men had been wounded.

To my great annoyance, Sergeant Cuff forbade me to accompany him when he and his officers set off for the scene in their police wagon. Believe me, hauling yourself up on to the driver's box is a hard enough task for someone of my height even when the vehicle's stationary; when the horses are being whipped into a frenzy, as they were when the wagon pulled away, it's a feat of the most extreme gymnastics. It felt exhilarating, though. You should have seen the driver's face when I suddenly appeared at his side!

Through Cornhill, Cheapside, Ludgate, Fleet Street,

the wind whipped through my hair, for I hadn't had a chance to change back into my own clothes, let alone grab my hat. Up Drury Lane and down Long Acre we flew, till the driver pulled the horses up short just shy of St Martin's Lane. I ducked down out of sight as Sergeant Cuff and his men jumped out of the covered wagon, then I lowered myself to the ground and took chase. I could hear the muffled sound of gunfire echoing through the streets, punctuated by a man's bellowing screams. The screams turned out to be from the pub's landlord; blood gushing from his shoulder, the great bear of a fellow was staggering round in circles outside his own establishment. Ignoring his distress, Cuff's men charged at the doors. Needless to say I was hot on their heels.

Inside, too terrified to move, a handful of late-night patrons sat staring at the body of a man lying on the sawdust-covered floor. I glanced at it in passing and was pleased to see that it wasn't anyone I knew.

So far my presence had gone unnoticed. Even in the corridor at the top of the stairs, I managed to evade the sergeant's vigilant gaze by falling in behind the stout, trusty officer at the back of the line. Almost immediately there came a rapid succession of shots. Everybody ducked as they blew away yet another section of the door's riddled panelling.

'As far as we can tell, he's in there alone, but he has more than two pistols at his disposal,' explained one of the men who'd been sent there originally. 'Four, possibly five, I believe.'

'Then it will take him some time to reload them,'

remarked the sergeant. 'We'll storm the room after his next volley. Men, charge your weapons.'

Everyone set to work with their powder and pellets. Sure enough, before very long Johnny started firing again. I counted the blasts, along with every other man in that corridor. One. Two. Three. A pause. Four. Was there a fifth pistol or not? The seconds ticked by.

Holding his hand up to restrain his men, Sergeant Cuff cried, 'Ready men? Go!' He kicked open what remained of the door but, like everyone else, he held his ground. A fifth shot rang out, followed closely by a sixth, taking away two solid chunks of the door frame.

'Charge!'

We piled through the doorway amid a flurry of gun-fire, all of it our own. After the initial confusion, I realized the room was empty.

'He's gone,' said the sergeant, making a quick but careful search of the room.

I ran to the open window and looked down.

Sergeant Cuff joined me a second later, too late to see what I'd seen: the look of fury in Johnny's eyes as he clambered to his feet and quickly limped away; a look of fury that was directed at me.

'Well, what are you waiting for?' cried the sergeant to his men. 'Get down there and hunt him out!'

Though they searched the neighbouring streets and buildings for close on an hour, they found no sign of him. Johnny was gone.

The surprises of that Wednesday evening were not over for me yet, however. Back in my own clothes at last, I arrived home late at my lodgings only to find Julius and Bertha entertaining company. Seated with them at the table, braving the heat with his fingers to cram small amounts of steaming potato into his mouth, was the boy I had last seen in Twickenham, who'd been posing as the Maharajah of Lahore. He was thinner, his face unwashed and his clothes dishevelled, yet still a spark of devilment managed to shine through.

'Your Highness,' I greeted him with a nod of the head, 'for I confess I know not what else to call you…'

'My name is really Sandeep,' he replied, in his rich, sing-song voice. 'Sandeep Singh—though I'm no relation to His Highness,' he added quickly, when he saw the look of consternation on my face. 'All Sikh boys are given the name Singh. It's our tradition. But most people call me Mutari, which in my language means Magpie. They call me this because there is no fleeter-of-foot, less-likely-to-be-caged pickpocket in all of Lahore.'

I had to stop myself from gasping at the boy's out-and-out cheek. *The impudence* of the fellow! *The audacity*! *The sheer brass neck*! Personal vanities aside, the lad's skills were really no match for mine.

'How did you find me, Sandeep?'

'Well,' he said, laying the potato aside and settling down, as if to recount a lengthy story, 'when I over-heard Treech plotting to destroy the daguerreotype by burning down your employer's bank, I knew it was my duty to escape. So I made my way to London on foot, keeping to the quieter lanes and byways. The days were cold, and the nights even colder. When the sun went down, I sought refuge in farmers' barns. But the words I remembered you saying spurred me on, how you lived on the Caledonian Road, near where they are building a new railway terminus. It should not be too hard to find this place, I imagined, but each time I ask for directions, people notice the colour of my skin and remark upon it, and I realize I am putting myself in danger. And when I do eventually find this place, it turns out to be such a godless spot! *Aieee!* I see drovers herding cattle to the slaughter by their dozens. Dozens! In spite of this I force myself to sit by the side of the road, and I wait and watch. And when, after many hours have passed, I spy this young man here trudging his weary way homeward, I approach him, for it cannot be a matter of coincidence that he shares the same eyes as you, Gooseberry—or should I say Octavius?'

Julius beamed.

'When I explained how I knew you,' Sandeep continued, 'your brother was kind enough to take me in and, as you can see, he and your good friend Bertha have been entertaining me lavishly by showing me their wonderful new photographic portraits and providing me with much needed sustenance.'

'Lad's as skinny as a rake,' grunted Bertha. 'Needs feedin' up. Been tellin' us about the plan to steal some whopper of a diamond, 'e has.'

'Yes,' said Sandeep, 'my one consolation in this whole business is that I—and I alone—have foiled Mr Treech's plot. Without me he cannot hope to make the planned substitution.'

Hmmm. What did I tell you? Sheer brass neck. 'Actually,

Sandeep, Treech is dead,' I informed him, enjoying the moment. 'His superior shot him, either out of rage or simply to tie up loose ends.'

The boy stared at me in alarm. 'But the maharajah, he is safe?'

'I believe so, yes. One of the gang took him into hiding quite some time ago. As for the substitution, they found another way to do it.' I went on to relate the evening's events, much to everyone's delight— even Sandeep's, to give him his due—though Bertha looked somewhat down-in-the-mouth when I revealed that not only had Josiah Hook—the man he knew as the Client—flown the coop, but Johnny Knight was in the wind, too. 'The question is,' I concluded, 'where do we go from here?'

'Nowhere,' muttered Bertha despondently. 'I can't go bleedin' nowhere till Johnny's caught.'

'I have been thinking,' said Sandeep, 'this your friend of yours, this Sergeant Cuff. Perhaps I should meet him and explain my side of the story. Maybe it will be of help.'

'You can take it from me, it don't do no good to go blabbing your screech off to no law,' advised Bertha, as he poked one final log into the stove. 'That's wot comes from ruminatin' 'bout things too late at night.'

'It really depends,' I said, 'on whether or not you were ever a willing accomplice.'

'A willing accomplice?' Sandeep looked horrified at the very suggestion. 'Do you imagine for one moment that I *wanted* my face to be cut? Or that I wished any harm to come to the maharajah? The hopes and dreams of the whole Sikh nation rest with him.'

'Then why did you do it? Why go along with them?'

'I was given a choice between that and prison,' he said simply.

So much for the legendary Magpie, the fleetest-of-foot, least-likely-to-be-caged pickpocket in all of Lahore, I thought.

Aloud I said, 'All right, I'll see what I can do to arrange a meeting.'

I noticed Julius nodding off in his chair so, after resolving the increasingly-cramped sleeping arrangements, we all bedded down for the night.

Given the happenings of the past two days, Thursday felt rather flat by comparison—apart from one small incident, that is. I needed to consult Mr James, Miss Penelope's beau, as to how best to communicate to his brother that it was now safe for him and his guests—the maharajah and his guardian—to make their return. When I arrived at the Montagu Square house, it was Mr Betteredge who answered the door. Having explained my business to him, I expected to be shown up to Mr James's room. Instead he stood there waiting and looking down at me expectantly.

A whole minute must have ticked by before he eventually asked, 'May I take your hat, son?'

'My…*hat*?' I wasn't sure I'd heard him correctly.

'Your hat,' he said. I swear on my life that I didn't shed a single tear, yet I was so overwhelmed that he quickly added, 'Would the young master care to be shown to a room where he can compose himself?'

By two in the afternoon, I was leaning against a tree close to Hyde Park's Cumberland Gate. That particular position afforded me an unobstructed view of the park bench under which James and Thomas left notes for each other. There was a note for Thomas there now, that James had penned at my request. Though it was a chilly day, there was still a steady stream of people keen to take the fresh air. As I watched, a man detached himself from a group that had just entered and sat himself down on the bench. His face hidden beneath a swaddling of scarves, he slowly glanced left and right, then casually reached under the bench. Locating the note I'd placed there, he opened it, read it, and looked up in surprise. I smiled and waved. For a minute I thought he might bolt.

'Please do not make me run after you, sir,' I begged him as I approached. 'What your brother says is true. Sir Humphrey Mallard is in custody. The plot to steal the diamond has failed.'

'And the boy standing by the tree is someone I can trust with my life?' he added sceptically, referring to the final paragraph on the sheet of paper.

'Yes, Mr Thomas, you can. My name is Octavius, though most people call me Gooseberry. I'm here to see that you and those you protect get safely home.'

He took some convincing, I must say, but in the end he agreed to accompany me back to the Blakes' house for a *tête-à-tête* with his brother.

Next I paid a visit to the good Sergeant Cuff, in the hope of learning his intentions regarding Thomas and Sandeep, as there was a distinct possibility that both might be viewed as co-conspirators in Mallard's scheme. Disappointed, though not entirely surprised by the result, I found I had one more journey to make before taking a cab back to my lodgings. I needed to deliver a letter, one that I'd had the foresight to compose during my brief time at the Blakes'. I was going to miss travelling like this, I reflected, as the cab rolled its way through the London streets; I'd become very used to this most expedient form of transport.

I arrived at work on Friday at the normal time, only to be taunted again by Mr Grayling as I went to collect my final *per diem* and—by comparison—my rather paltry wages for the week. This time I was ready for him. When he started on about my eyes, I took a crumpled ball of paper from my pocket and tossed it on to his desk. Mr Grayling—or *Misss*-ter *Chrisss*-topher, as I'd decided to call him, for it could be delivered with a large measure of insolence by the simple expedient of elongating the first syllable of each word—blanched and fell silent.

Sandeep, who I'd brought with me, turned to me and asked in Mr Christopher's hearing, 'Is that the fool of a clerk who gave you your nickname?' When I agreed that it was, he added, 'Well, well. You certainly seem to have the situation well in control.' Perhaps I had misjudged the boy after all.

George and George couldn't stop themselves gawking at Sandeep as I led him along to Mr Bruff's office.

'I wouldn't do that, if I was you,' the older George warned me as I went to knock, a kindness that earned him a punch on the arm from his younger colleague. 'Mr Bruff's got some bigwig from Scotland Yard with him,' he carried on, despite it. 'He won't like you barging in.'

'It's all right,' I assured him. 'It was me who invited

the sergeant here. He's keen to meet my friend, Sandeep.'

'Hello there, my name's George,' said George, offering Sandeep his hand. The younger George took exception to this and dug his friend in the ribs with his elbow. As the pair shook hands, I explained that my companion had once been the Maharajah of Lahore—which wasn't *entirely* untrue—much to the older George's delight and the younger George's huffy disappointment.

When we finally entered the office, we found Sergeant Cuff and Mr Bruff reminiscing about their parts in the Moonstone affair, with two of the sergeant's men in attendance, respectfully looking on. That put the wind up me, I'm not ashamed to say. The fact that there were two of them seemed significant. Mr Bruff's mouth dropped open as I ushered Sandeep into his presence. Worryingly, Sergeant Cuff's did not.

For quite some days now I'd been keeping Mr Bruff in the dark about my various activities. Though once again he was brimming with questions, I managed to stave them off by promising to reveal everything as soon as we got to the Blakes'. At my request, he retrieved the daguerreotype from his safe and, without further ado, we all set off.

It was Samuel, the footman, who once more answered the door to us. He took Mr Bruff's hat quite willingly, and then deigned to take the sergeant's. The sergeant's two men, however, he pointedly ignored. As Mr Bruff led the way to the library, he then turned to me.

'You hat, sir?' he asked. If the judgemental young Samuel was prepared to take my hat, I had certainly come up in the world. I smiled as I handed it to him, then followed my employer in.

With the addition of Mr James, who I had finally forgiven for attempting to cut my throat, everyone in the household was present, just as they had been on that previous Monday, when we'd first been summoned to attend. Though they greeted Sergeant Cuff warmly enough—for it was some two or three years since they had last seen him—the warmest reception they reserved for me.

'Is this who I think it is?' Mrs Blake whispered in my ear, as she stole up behind me. She'd been regarding Sandeep with an almost reverential stare ever since we'd entered. Unfortunately he overheard her.

'My name is Sandeep,' he said, introducing himself, 'though most people call me Mutari, which in my language means Magpie, for there is no fleeter-of-foot—'

'No,' I hastily cut him short. 'It's not. But we'll get to him presently, I promise. You see, we're still waiting for people to arrive, miss.' Turning to my employer, I asked, 'What time is it, sir?'

Mr Bruff consulted his watch. 'Nearly half-past ten,' he replied.

'Mr Betteredge,' I said, 'I see you have your copy of *Robinson Crusoe* with you. While we wait, may I ask, has that excellent tome any guidance for us today?'

Eyeing the sergeant and his men warily from his seat by the fire, the elderly servant nodded, cleared his throat, and read, '"...*if they were sent to England, they would all be hanged in chains, to be sure; but that if they would join in such an attempt as to recover the ship, he would have the governor's engagement for their pardon*." For their pardon, sir. For their pardon.'

It really was uncanny what the man could do with that book of his. He was better than a gypsy fortune teller in a caravan. My thoughts were interrupted, however, as Samuel entered the room. He was looking decidedly shaken.

'A Mr Thomas Shepherd and a Dr John Login to see you, sir,' he announced. 'And…and…and…'

'And *what?*' asked Mr Blake.

My hopes rose, only to fall again as Samuel replied, 'Well, some poor, thin wretch of a lad who claims to be the Maharajah of Lahore.'

CHAPTER EIGHTEEN

THE THREE MEN—WELL, two men and a boy, to be precise—who shuffled nervously into the library were clearly in a state of nervous exhaustion. They were so thin that their filthy, tattered garments hung from their bones as if from a peg. Their complexions were sallow and their skin was caked with grime.

James struggled to his feet and went to embrace his brother. Thomas's companion—Dr Login, I presumed—gasped and rubbed his eyes as Sandeep raced forward to shake the maharajah by the hand. His surprise was amply justified, as each boy was the mirror image of the other—literally the mirror image, for while Sandeep's scar ran down the right side of his face, the maharajah's ran down his left.

The maharajah was also taken aback. 'Who *are* you?' he asked, gawking at the twin who stood before him.

'Your Highness, I am Sandeep Singh, though most people call me Mutari—'

'Mutari?' Suddenly the maharajah's features became

just as animated as his double's. '*You're* Mutari? The Magpie? The fleetest-of-foot, least-likely-to-be-caged pickpocket in all of Lahore? Why, I have heard many fascinating tales of your exploits!'

Oh, really!

'Come,' the boy continued, 'I would have a demonstration of your talents. I will stand here and you will try to steal something from me.'

'Excuse me,' I butted in, only to find myself being ignored by the pair of them.

'Why would I do such a disreputable thing, Your Highness?' asked Sandeep, looking anxious and bewildered.

The maharajah shrugged. 'Because I command you to? Surely that is reason enough.'

As Sandeep bowed his head in acceptance, his hand darted out. I quickly slapped it aside before it could breach the maharajah's jacket. Both boys turned to me and stared.

'Enough of this! I didn't bring you here for this nonsense! Mr Bruff, what time is it, sir?'

'It's twenty minutes to eleven by my watch. Why?'

I glanced at the library doors, which Samuel, the footman, had closed on his departure. They hadn't budged. 'Perhaps we should get started,' I said, for people were getting restless. 'May I have the daguerreotype, please?' Mr Bruff rummaged about in his pocket and handed it to me.

'I know that one or other of these boys is the subject of that accursed portrait,' Mrs Blake's aunt declared loudly. 'If I were to hazard a guess, I'd say it was the one who arrived first.'

'You would think so, wouldn't you, miss,' I said, holding up the photograph in question beside Sandeep's face. 'But the fact is, due to the very nature of the process, a daguerreotype is always laterally reversed.'

Although I had everyone's attention, I didn't get the reaction I was hoping for. Only Dr Login and one of Sergeant Cuff's officers nodded sagely—though, in the case of the officer, I strongly suspected he was doing so in order to impress his boss. Everyone else was still looking to me for an explanation.

'They're mirror images,' I said, as I took my own daguerreotype from my pocket and gave it to Mr Blake to pass around. Sighs of comprehension echoed round the room as, one by one, people saw the portrait where I was holding up a sheet of paper. The words *"The scar should be on the left, not on the right"* were mirrored, of course. 'Which leads me to believe that Cyrus Treech had never set eyes on the real maharajah when he took his knife to Sandeep. He was working from the photograph that was later found in Mrs Merridew's bag.'

'Speaking of eyes,' Mrs Blake's aunt interjected as she studied my portrait, 'whoever took this picture has certainly done justice to yours.'

'Aunt Merridew, it might be best if we stick to the point,' Mrs Blake admonished her gently.

'All he says is true,' said Sandeep. 'Mr Treech was simply a lowly surgeon. When I was arrested on the streets of Lahore last year, he came to me and gave me the choice of working for him or staying in prison. Even when he said he must cut my cheek, I did not flinch, for it is a well known fact that, in Lahore, people meet their deaths in prison. I remember all too well how he needed to consult the daguerreotype many times before he wielded his razor.'

'But Treech was unaware that daguerreotypes are laterally reversed,' I pointed out. 'In his own dying words, he *"picked the wrong side"*.'

Mrs Blake shifted uneasily in her chair. 'I still don't understand,' she said, inclining her head to acknowledge the maharajah, 'what these people were hoping to gain by replacing His Highness with a double.'

'They were after the Kohinoor diamond, madam,' replied Sandeep. 'It used to belong to the maharajah, and to his father before him. How natural it would be, when the stone is presented to be re-cut, if His Highness requests to hold it one last time. They chose me to play the part, not just because I look like His Highness, but because there is no fleeter-of-foot, less-likely-to-be-caged—'

'They chose him because he had the skills to exchange the stone for a replica!' I snapped. '*Absolute child's play*!' I added, under my breath. '*A toddler of four could have done it*!'

'So by this point,' said Mrs Blake, feeling her way through the narrative, 'His Highness had already been taken prisoner?'

'Yes,' Sandeep replied. 'After many weeks of healing, Mr Treech and I boarded a boat bound for England. By the time we arrived at the East India Docks, Josiah Hook, his partner in crime, had kidnapped the maharajah and his guardian and removed them to one of the asylum's outlying farms, to clear the way for me. I never got to meet His Highness. They made sure they kept us apart.'

'Hook needed someone to watch over the pair,' I took up the story again, 'someone who was ambitious enough to stay the course, so he roped in his junior colleague, Mr James's brother, Thomas. As far as it was possible, though, they kept Thomas in the dark. Mr James's brother knew nothing of the diamond, and he'd been warned that his prisoners would make false claims as to their identities.' I had no idea if this was true, but I knew that, as things stood, it would be Thomas's best and only defence.

'That's not strictly the case,' piped up Thomas, right on cue. *Trust the people you're trying to save to go and put their foot in it.* I threw him a warning glance—as did James—but he took no notice of either of us. 'I knew exactly who these people were,' he admitted.

'Be that as it may,' I said, 'you didn't know what Hook and Mallard were planning, and when you found out that your charges were to be murdered, you took them into hiding—and with them, the daguerreotype. You kept them safe at considerable risk to yourself.'

'I can attest to that,' Dr Login avowed.

Trembling and overwrought, Thomas appeared to be on the verge of tears. 'Well, yes,' he said, lowering his head, 'I suppose if you care to put it that way…'

'Where?' I said.

Thomas looked up, his face perplexed.

'Where did you hide them?' I clarified. 'Your brother couldn't tell me, and it's the one thing I couldn't figure out for myself.'

'Oh…there's a warehouse…a large one…not too

far from Hyde Park. It's where they store the sections of glass that made up the Crystal Palace. The guard on the gate was a friend of my late father.'

'Sir, your actions helped save two innocent lives.' I was trying not to lay it on too thick, for I knew that Sergeant Cuff was unlikely to be taken in by such sentimental tricks. Even so, Thomas received a round of applause led by Mr Blake. One of the sergeant's officers joined in and I saw the sergeant glowering at him. It was not a good sign. 'Mr Bruff, what time do you have, sir?'

'Must you keep asking me to consult my timepiece, Gooseberry?' my employer answered sharply. 'It's coming up for eleven of the clock, if you must know.'

Nearly eleven, and still the doors remained closed, yet it seemed I had little choice but to carry on.

'Thomas was not the only hero,' I continued. 'When Sandeep thought the daguerreotype was about to be destroyed, he too tried to thwart Mallard's plans. He managed to escape from Treech, then he came to London.'

Sandeep beamed at me. 'Yes, carefully—oh, so carefully—I made my way to London on foot, keeping to the quieter lanes and byways. The days were cold, and the nights even colder. When the sun went down, shivering to the very marrow of my bones, I sought refuge in—'

Oh, enough! 'Undaunted, Sir Humphrey Mallard, the brains behind it all, came up with a different plot,' I ploughed on, leaving Sandeep to flounder. 'He enlisted the help of Johnny Knight, the deranged head of London's underworld. Sergeant Cuff, would you care to do the honours and take up the story?'

A trace of a smile crept across the sergeant's weather-beaten face. 'Really? When you're doing such a fine job spinning the tale? I'm afraid my poor contribution would seem dull and disappointing by comparison,' he said dryly.

'Please, sir. I'm sure the Blakes and their guests would much prefer to hear the official version of what happened. After all, it occurred on your watch.'

'Do you mean to tell us the blackguard went through with it, Cuff?' cried Mr Blake, aghast. 'This Mallard chap *stole* the Kohinoor diamond?'

By now Sergeant Cuff was fielding questions from all sides.

'Very well, very well!' he conceded, holding his hands up in surrender.

As he started into his story, I kept my eyes on the doors, willing them to open, but they stubbornly remained shut. Had I made a dreadful mistake? *Could Robinson Crusoe possibly be wrong for once?* Eleven o'clock came and went. Another five minutes crawled by, then ten—by which point the sergeant was reaching his nail-biting climax—Johnny firing volleys of shots through the door, then leaping to his freedom through the window.

'There have been no sightings of this Johnny Knight character,' the sergeant concluded, 'nor of Josiah Hook, but I'm confident we'll get them both in the end. The Yard always gets their man.'

This, too, received a round of applause. Only the officer who'd been taken to task over clapping for Thomas remained perfectly still; his blank expression didn't waver. Once again he received a look from the sergeant for his poor sense of judgement.

'Unfortunately, that brings me to my purpose here today,' intoned Sergeant Cuff in his deep bass voice. 'Sandeep Singh, Mr Thomas Shepherd, it is my solemn if unpleasant duty to place you both under arrest.'

The protests came fast and furious. Miss Penelope rushed to Mr James's side as he tried to prevent one of the sergeant's men from reaching his brother. Dr Login also joined the fray—although, in his weakened condition, his feeble, doddering efforts were of little use. Cuff's other man was faring no better. To get to Sandeep, he had to go through the Maharajah of Lahore, who was sticking to his fellow countryman— and, dare I say it? *hero*—like a rabid guard dog. The officer clearly had some notion that the lad was royalty, and that laying his hands on him would constitute a transgression. Sergeant Cuff was having a time of it, too, responding as best he could to Mr Bruff's and Mr Blake's demands to see the warrant. That wasn't even the worst of it for him, for he found himself on the receiving end of Mrs Blake's sharp tongue. Eventually he took a whistle from his jacket pocket, and blew it as loudly and as long as his breath would allow. The shrill, piercing note halted everyone in their tracks.

'IT IS USELESS FOR THESE MEN TO RESIST ARREST,' he bellowed. 'THEY ARE CRIMINALS AND, AS SUCH, THEY *WILL* BE BROUGHT TO JUSTICE. AID THEM IN THEIR ENDEAVOUR AND I SHALL HAVE NO CHOICE BUT TO ARREST YOU, TOO!'

Slowly, unwillingly, Sandeep's and Thomas's protectors stepped aside, allowing Cuff's men access to their quarry.

'What time is it, please, Mr Bruff?' I asked, as the doors to the library finally parted and a truly speechless Samuel appeared. I didn't hear his indignant reply, for I was too busy watching the jabbering footman.

'What is it, Samuel? What's the matter?' asked Mr Blake.

But Samuel's tongue failed him. 'Sir…sir…sir…' was all he managed to say, as a figure materialized behind him in the doorway and strode breezily into the room.

'Ah, Octavius, my good friend. I apologize for the lateness of my arrival, sir. My wife, she has had an extremely busy morning.'

The stunned silence was broken only by the crackle of logs on the fire and the snoring of old Mr Betteredge asleep in his chair. Everyone stood eyeing the visitor with their mouths open wide.

'Hello there, Your Royal Highness,' I greeted my visitor. 'Thank you for coming. I knew you wouldn't want the honour of two good men to be brought into disrepute.'

Prince Albert gave me a glorious smile. "'*Sir*" should suffice between friends, should it not? So where are these stalwarts of moral perfection? I believe introductions are in order.'

'This is Sandeep Singh, sir. And this is the Maharajah of Lahore.' I noted the look of shock on the prince's face, presumably from seeing double. The officer holding Sandeep mistook it for displeasure and immediately let go of the boy.

'Sandeep chose to abscond rather than to co-operate with Sir Humphrey Mallard,' I added quickly, before he went and ruined it all by trying to introduce himself, 'effectively foiling his plot. I'm afraid he doesn't speak English too well.' I could see that Sandeep was about to object, so I did the one thing I could—I stamped on his foot.

'*Ouch*! Why did you go and do that?'

'As I said, sir, he doesn't speak English too well. And these men over here are Mr Thomas Shepherd and Dr Login. Mr Thomas risked his own life to save the maharajah and the doctor.'

'He did, Your Royal Highness,' declared Dr Login, speaking in Thomas's defence. 'But now this preposterous policeman plans to arrest him—him and the poor boy they disfigured.'

The prince followed the doctor's glance as it fell on Sergeant Cuff. Sergeant Cuff gazed back quite impassively.

'Is this true, Sergeant?'

'It is, Your Highness. The pair were involved in Mallard's scheme.'

'Then it is a good thing I have royal pardons for them both, signed this very morning by my wife's fair hand.'

The sergeant nodded gracefully. Then he pursed his lips and said to me, 'Well played, Gooseberry. Decidedly well played.'

Prince Albert stayed longer than I'd anticipated. Though he was clearly charmed by Mrs Blake, who was bemoaning the fact that her entire household seemed to be cursed by diamonds, his accent returned every time Mr Blake attempted to talk about politics. When Mr Betteredge finally woke up, he was so affected by finding Prince Albert there in the room with him that his daughter had to administer a restorative drink. His book had fallen on the floor while he slept, open at a page roughly a quarter of the way in. I wandered over, curious to see what it had to say:

"It would have made a stoic smile, to have seen me and my little family sit down to dinner: there was my majesty, the prince and lord of the whole island…"

*Note to self: find out what sort of animal a stoic is. Could it perchance be a misprint? Was the writer in fact talking about "*stoats*"?*

As I made my way back to my lodgings that evening—without Sandeep, I hasten to add, for he'd chosen to make his home with the maharajah—I reflected that having to walk places wasn't such a terrible ordeal. You could always rely on your own two feet to get you to your destination eventually. Being a Friday, I stopped at Mrs Grogan's to pick up a selection of pies, some ginger beer, and a nice roasted fowl for our supper. Even though we would now have to cut our cloth accordingly, as the saying goes, I thought we all deserved a good blow out.

Neither Bertha nor Julius was there when I arrived home, but it wasn't long before Bertha returned, carrying a basket of firewood and a string bag of potatoes.

'Where are you getting all this?' I asked, aware that Bertha had no money of his own.

'Bloke with the stall on the corner of Rodney Street,' he sniffed. ''E gives it me.'

'*Gives* it to you?'

'You heard.'

I thought about it for a moment and decided it was best not to pursue the matter.

'A note came for you,' said Bertha, as he stacked the firewood in the crate. ''S'on the table.'

I picked up the envelope and opened it. Inside were two sheets of paper, both yellowed with age.

My heart chilled to ice in a single beat.

Scrawled in pencil in Julius's laboured writing, with too many C's, and not enough N's or S's, the first sheet contained just one word. Our panic word.

Unnecessary.

CHAPTER NINETEEN

"*UNECCESARY*".

I forced myself to read the accompanying sheet.

"*Thames Tunnel. Tomorrow night. Come alone if you don't want Sprat's last smile to be the one I carve into his throat.*"

'Wot does it say?' asked Bertha, having noticed the strained silence. He'd finished stacking the last of the firewood and was leaning back, straightening his spine.

'Bertha, did you tell anyone about Julius?'

'Wot?'

'Did you tell anyone about Julius?'

'I ain't told no one about no one. Why? Wot's the note say?'

'You must have told someone.'

'Nah! I gave you me word I wouldn't, and I ain't.'

His answer seemed genuine enough, but who else would know where Julius worked? Who else would refer to him as *Sprat*?

'What about your friend who gives you the firewood? Ever mention Julius to him?'

'Nah. To be honest, we don't talk that much. Now, tell me wot that note says.'

I held out the one from Julius for him to examine.

'This is Sprat's 'and writin',' he concluded, his dark, bushy eyebrows knitting into a frown. 'Wot's 'e doin' sending you notes? Wot's it say?'

'It says, "*unnecessary*".'

'Unnecessary? Ain't that the word wot you used that night when you went to the Bucket of Blood? If you didn't come back, like, I was meant to pass it on to Julius?'

'It's our panic word, Bertha.'

'Panic word?'

'If I ever found myself in real trouble, all I had to do was say the word in Julius's hearing, and he'd know to make a dash for it. After that, he had a list of instructions to keep him safe.'

Bertha grunted. 'So wot's 'e doin' writing it to you, then?'

'He's telling me he's in trouble.'

'*Trouble*?' Bertha's pock-marked face clouded over as I read out the accompanying letter. 'Oh, Octopus, I swear to you I didn't tell no one! I swear it on me old ma's grave! May she come back and cut me bleedin' tongue out if I so much as tell you a word of a lie!'

'Then how did Johnny find him? How, Bertha?'

Bertha gave this some thought. Suddenly he slapped the middle of his forehead with the heel of his palm. 'Oh, Gawd, oh, Gawd, oh, Gawd!' he squawked. 'It's all 'cause of that blasted nickname I give him…and the fact I been callin' you Octopus. 'E wanted to call you that, too, see?'

Unfortunately, I did.

'The lad's been usin' both 'em names on the fish stall. Johnny must've put feelers out, and somebody who'd 'eard 'im went and grassed 'im up. Oh, Gawd, if anything happens to him, I'll never forgive meself!' A look of grim determination fixed itself stubbornly to his face. 'So wot's the plan? Wot we gunna do?'

'*We* aren't going to do anything. It's me who Johnny wants. If it means he'll free Julius, he can have me.'

'For such a smart lad, you really can be as dense as two short planks. This is Johnny we're talking about. Yeh can't trust Johnny as far as yeh can throw 'im. We need a plan. We need a plan.'

Bertha was right.

'Is there *anything* Johnny's afraid of?' I asked.

Bertha shook his head. 'Nah. 'E ain't afraid of nothin'. Well, nothin', that is, 'cept cats.'

'*Cats*?'

'I caught him one time, down this alley, right, cowering—*cowering*, I tell you—in front of this big black cat. I just figured 'e were superstitious, like. Didn't let him see me there—he'd of killed me if he 'ad—and I sure as 'ell kept quiet about it, after.'

'Cats?' I said again.

'Well, it's somefin', ain't it?'

Yes, it was something, but I sincerely doubted it would be enough. Between us we ate a miserable supper then, though the last thing I felt like was sleep, I spread out my bed-roll and lay down to get some rest. The hours of the night crept past at a snail's pace, and it was only when the patch of sky through the window had paled from a vivid Indian ink to a dark sludge-grey that I finally dozed off.

When I awoke some time later, the room was awash with watery sunlight. I glanced about, looking for Bertha, but it seemed he'd taken himself off out while I slept. I got up and sat at the table. Beside the remains of the previous night's meal Bertha had laid out half a dozen or so sturdy knives. I tried each of them in my hand to see how it felt. In all honesty, they all felt foreign.

The day wore on, and Bertha failed to reappear. As evening fell, I pocketed two of the knives and went in search of a cab.

Considering the tunnel was meant to be closed, it was attracting its fair share of visitors. I'd been standing in the doorway of one of the surrounding warehouses, keeping watch on the building for a little under an hour. People were coming and going, just as they did during the day. *If I only knew what I was walking into*, I reasoned, *I would be able to prepare myself better*. But I did know what I was walking into. I was walking into a trap.

Realizing that these negative thoughts were not helping to set Julius free, I stowed one of the knives in a sheath in my boot and set off inside.

There was no one in the ticket booth; in fact, the octagonal room was deserted. The door to the shaft stood open and, through it, I could see the flicker of firelight around the walls. Cautiously, I stuck my head round the doorway and peered down at the circular floor below.

It had certainly seen some changes. At its centre

there now stood a boxing ring, flanked at each corner by a blazing metal drum. Stripped to the waist, two men were pitting themselves against each other in a bare-knuckled bout. As the blood flew, the crowd of onlookers screeched and bayed their approval. On the marble counter top between the two tunnel entrances, Johnny Knight sat perched on a chair, ruling over this grisly empire like a king. Beside him, to his left, stood Colin, Eric's twin brother. It appeared that, since Eric's arrest, Colin had been promoted to the lofty position of deuce—not that he looked happy about it. His face couldn't have been more miserable. On the counter, to Johnny's right, stood Mallard's young conspirator, Hook.

I crept down the spiral steps to the first landing, which afforded me a view of the opposite side of the room. I spied Julius in the alcove normally reserved for the monkey, gagged and bound to a stake, but seemingly unharmed…and seemingly unguarded.

Keeping to the shadows, I made my way down. At the bottom, I blended in with the throng. The heat from the burning drums had everyone sweating, so the smell of human bodies was overpowering as I jostled through the crowd. Julius, who hadn't seen me coming, gave a little start as I suddenly appeared.

'Keep very quiet,' I whispered, as I began to pull his gag off. He nodded in response. 'I'm going to have to cut you free, so stand still as you can for me, all right?' Another nod.

I started with his feet, then moved slowly up the pole, hacking through the ropes just as fast as I could.

'Octavius…'

'Shhh!'

'No, Octavius, you need to look…'

I turned my head and saw Colin and Hook dashing towards me. The crowd were parting before them like the Red Sea. Even the two opponents in the ring had ceased their fighting. They were standing and gawping at us like everyone else. Behind them, on his throne, Johnny let out a shriek of laughter.

'Well, well, well,' he crowed. 'Look who's come to join us. Colin, get his knife off him, then search him.'

Colin grabbed me by the wrist, tugged the knife out of my hand, and gave me a thorough patting down.

'And his boots. Take his boots.'

Hook held me in an arm-lock as Colin removed first one and then the other. When he came across the second blade, he held it high, like he'd found himself a trophy.

'Forget the blade,' ordered Johnny. 'Hold up the boots.'

Colin seemed surprised, but did as he was asked.

'It was me,' said Johnny, 'all those years ago. It was me what took your boots.'

'Really?' I replied, though it was something I'd suspected all along. 'Then it's you I have to thank, Johnny.'

'Thank?'

'Why, yes. If it weren't for you, I'd still be up to my neck in the Life. You took my boots and Fortune smiled on me.'

Johnny frowned, then tried to laugh it off. 'And will Fortune smile on you once more, now that I get to take them all over again? See, that's what I'd call

Fate. And, as I see it, *Fate ain't no smilin' matter.*'

'Yet it's always served me well throughout the years. Can the same be said of you, Johnny? Apparently not.'

Again the frown. 'Enough of your damn philoso-phizing! You got any last words for your brother, Octopus? 'Cause I'm sure he's got some choice ones for you.'

I turned to Julius. He was trying to put a brave face on it, but I could see the tears starting to well up in his eyes.

'I'm truly sorry,' I said. 'I tried my best to protect you from all this, but I failed.'

'They told me you're a pickpocket,' he snivelled. 'Is that true, Octavius? Are you a pickpocket?'

'Julius—'

'Please…I need to know.'

'Yes, Julius. I am. Or, at least, I was.'

'A pickpocket? A *pickpocket?*'

Julius hung his head. Initially I thought it was because he couldn't bring himself to look at me, but then I realized he was actually staring at his trouser pocket. I gave it a brief glance, too. When they'd taken Julius from the fish stall, they hadn't bothered to search him. He was still carrying his gutting knife. *Oh, well done, Julius!* I placed one hand on my brother's shoulder and hugged him to me.

'You two make me sick!' cried Johnny. 'Throw Octopus in the ring! We'll make the small fry watch as the little beggar dies!'

Colin took one arm and Hook the other, and together they dragged me across the floor and hurled me face-down into the blood-spattered ring. As I sprang to my feet, the two men, who five minutes before had been knocking each other senseless, eased themselves out through the ropes and into the audience. Johnny rose and leapt lithely to the ground.

'*Fight! Fight! Fight!*' came the call from all round, as he bounded into the ring to join me. At first we simply circled each other, as if testing each other's mettle, then, when he finally threw himself at me, I ducked to the side to try and dodge him. My foot slipped in blood and I promptly landed on my bottom. A roar of laughter went up from the crowd. Johnny, as vain as ever, held up his hands and cried, 'I didn't even touch the runt!'

My eyes were level with his boots at this point. As he paraded round the ring, I spied the hilt of a knife protruding from one of them: the right one. Then he made a serious error. Having milked my fall for all it was worth, he proceeded to plant a swift kick in my kidney. I caught hold of his boot just before impact and I didn't let go. It deadened the blow a little, and it gave me access to the knife. A quick tug had him sprawling on the ground beside me.

As I scrambled to my feet with his blade in my hand, I beheld a curious sight: Bertha, in his disguise, scurrying down the marble steps, carrying his bulging—and *heaving*—canvas bag. I had no time to ponder on this, however, for one angry, hissing Johnny was up-right once more, and coming at me with a knife that he'd pulled from his belt.

The blade swiped the air an inch from my stomach. I jumped back, only to find myself pressed against the ropes. Johnny lashed out again, catching the side of my wrist and sending my knife flying. The very next second, his went flying too, as Bertha appeared at the ringside and flung the contents of his bag in Johnny's face. Suddenly Johnny was fending off two furious, spitting cats.

Bertha's moment of glory was soon brought to an end when Hook threw himself at him and tackled him to the ground. The crowd, less sure about this turn of events, rapidly made way for the pair as they tussled back and forth across the floor. If Hook thought Bertha was easy game, he was mistaken. Bertha was laying into him with a rapid succession of close body-punches, while limiting his movements by clinging to him with his other arm.

By the time Johnny had pulled both the cats off his face, his skin was in bloody tatters. He wasn't trembling with feline fear, mind, but instead with pure, unfettered rage. He advanced on me slowly, backing me into a corner, where I could feel the lick of the flames on the back of my neck. I drew out Julius's gutting knife and held it out before me. Johnny lunged forward and grasped me by the wrist, wrenched the four-inch blade from my fingers, and tossed it blindly into the crowd. He hoisted me into the air like a bale of straw and hurled me across the ring. The next thing I knew, I was having the wind knocked out of me, as he landed, feet first, on my back.

'One of you bring me my god-damned chair!' he bawled. 'I need me some height if I'm going to grind this little worm into the ground!'

As I struggled up on all fours, I felt something

being pressed into my hand. My fingers closed around the solid, wooden handle of yet another knife. I looked up through the ropes and saw Colin, his mouth set in a thin, grim line.

'It's Eric's,' he muttered. 'My brother's going to swing for what he did, and all 'cause of Johnny bleedin' Knight. Kill him for me, Octopus. Kill him for me, right?'

Using the ropes, I hauled myself to my feet, and barely turned in time to see Johnny diving at me through the air, having launched himself from his chair. I staggered towards him and, in the very instant before our bodies collided, I raised the blade. That's all I did. His own weight and momentum drove it home as we hit the floor together.

Johnny's pale, colourless eyes grew wider. His breathing became ragged. All the fight went out of him at once. There was a look of profound bafflement upon his scratched and bloodied face, a look that froze and never altered. It was almost as if he were posing for a photograph. A daguerreotype of Johnny Knight, dead, burned into my brain for ever.

As I scrambled out from under his corpse, Bertha appeared at the ringside. There was a considerable amount of blood around his mouth, though there was no way to tell whether it was his or whether it was Hook's. Otherwise he seemed breathless but unhurt.

'Go on,' he said, attempting to wipe some of the blood away, 'you go and take Sprat 'ome with yeh. I'll see to what needs doin' 'ere. Go on, Octopus, you go.'

Feeling sick to my stomach, I went.

THE EPILOGUE

THE INVITATIONS ARRIVED AT the office on Monday the second of February. Despite my bruised ribs, I'd struggled in to work in the afternoon to ask for a short leave of absence. They arrived just as I was pleading—and sadly losing—my case, for I couldn't exactly reveal the extent of my injuries, let alone say how I'd come by them. One letter was addressed to Mr Mathew Bruff, Solicitor, the other to Master Octavius Guy, Detective. *Detective*, no less. I knew they were important when Mr Bruff stopped in mid-sentence while explaining how he expected me not only to be in as usual the next day, but to be on time. He passed me mine, then sank into his chair and stared morbidly at his for several minutes. Never one to let the grass grow under my feet, I tore mine open. The letter inside read:

"The Master of the Household is Commanded by Her Majesty Queen Victoria to invite Master Octavius Guy and his family to an evening reception at Buckingham Palace on Friday, 6 February, at 7 o'clock."

Suffice it to say, when Mr Bruff finally plucked up the courage to open his, he readily agreed to my week's leave of absence.

'Wot the blinkin' 'ell am I gunna wear?' shrieked Bertha, when I read out the letter that night.

'Your disguise?' I suggested hopefully.

'Nah. It'll be a cold day in hell before I wear that damn thing again.'

'Then we'll buy you something.' Prince Albert had included a satisfying number of pound coins in my envelope along with a note suggesting that the money might help me defray any expenses. *There*, I thought, *was a man with a great command of even the most subtle of English phrases*.

Friday evening saw us in a cab, heading down Bird Cage Walk. Julius and I were dressed in identical jackets and bowler hats, though we'd both chosen different designs in waistcoats. Julius had been plagued by bad dreams all week, but the prospect of getting his first waistcoat and bowler had lifted his spirits no end. Bertha had opted for much the same as he usually wore, though at least the skirt, blouse, and shawl were clean, as were the primrose-coloured ribbons he'd affixed to his hair.

On arrival, we were shown into a long gallery, where we were told to wait in line. Mr and Mrs Blake were there; so, in fact, with the exception of villains, was everyone else involved with the case. We weren't kept waiting long. Presently the doors at the end opened and Queen Victoria entered, accompanied by her husband, the prince. Smiling, chatting, and shaking their guests hands, they slowly made their way down the line towards us.

'And this, my dear, is my good friend, Octavius,' said the prince, when they eventually reached my little band. 'It is he you have to thank for the safe return of your diamond.'

'Your Majesty.' I gave a stately bow that would have even warmed the heart of that fussy little steward from the East India Company. 'May I present my brother, Julius?'

'I know you,' said Julius brightly, as he shook her by the hand. 'You're the lady what's on all the coins. I'm learning me money, see?'

Hmmm…

It was impossible to tell what Bertha said to her— even for the Queen herself—for he gave a beautiful curtsey, pulled his shawl across his mouth, and began whispering whatever it was through the muffling folds of the wool. Old habits die hard, I guess. After repeatedly leaning in and applying her ear, Queen Victoria shrugged and moved on.

When the formalities were over, we were ushered into a large hall and people began to mingle. I noticed Mrs Blake's aunt peering suspiciously at Bertha, so I steered both him and Julius over to the other side of the room—straight into the path of Mr Bruff.

'And who is this?' asked my employer, looking down at Julius.

I knew this moment had been coming. 'This is my brother, Julius, sir. Julius, this is my employer, Mr Bruff.'

'How do you do, young man?' Mr Bruff offered him his hand.

Julius, speechless, stared up at Mr Bruff as if he was somehow even more important than the Queen. I suppose that's what comes of having the "*unnecessary*" catechism drilled into him for the past six years, with its strictures about my employer's rank.

Mr Bruff, alarmed by the boy's gawking silence, murmured, 'Carry on, carry on,' and beat a hasty retreat.

I left Julius in Bertha's care and sauntered over to the window, where Sergeant Cuff stood gazing out over the Quadrangle. On my appearance, he slowly turned his head.

'Gooseberry.' The sergeant gave a nod of greeting, but his voice remained cool.

'Sergeant Cuff.' I can do cool myself.

'Still no sign of Johnny Knight and his friend, I regret to say.'

I shrugged. 'Perhaps they fled the city. Perhaps they've gone abroad.'

'Perhaps.' The seconds ticked by. 'By a strange co-incidence, on Wednesday last, a wherryman pulled the bloated bodies of two young men from the river,' he remarked casually. 'Their faces had been beaten to a pulp.'

'Any identifying scars on their bodies? Any papers on their persons to suggest who they were?'

'None.'

'Curious.'

The sergeant pursed his lips. 'Is there anything you wish to tell me, Gooseberry?'

I put on my *innocent face*, raised my head, and met his steely eyes. 'I should like to be able to tell you that good has prevailed, Sergeant Cuff; that God in His infinite wisdom has seen fit to exact justice. I should like to tell you that everything is right with the world—so much so that, even as we speak, there's an entire colony of stoats looking on and smiling their heads off.' By the puzzled expression on the sergeant's face, I gathered I'd come a cropper with the last part of that sentence. 'But what would I know? I'm simply an office boy who's just starting out in life and keen to pursue his career.'

The sergeant smiled. 'And I'm an old man who's at the end of his, and yearning to place it behind him,' he remarked dryly. 'I shall go back to growing roses and getting under my good wife's feet when she's trying to clean the house. I shall end my days in contentment.' He reached into his coat pocket, extracted a card, and held it out for me to take.

'What's this?' I asked.

'My address in Dorking, if you ever need to pick these old brains of mine. And I've a feeling you will. Whenever I hear the word "*career*", I always think of rearing horses galloping wildly off into the sunset. Ha! You don't choose to run with a career, Octavius. It chooses to run with *you*.' With that snippet of advice, he bade me a fond farewell.

There's very little left to tell, except perhaps for two tiny things. Mr Blake's party came to power on the twenty-third of February—much to everyone's disappointment, I might add, apart from the land-owning farmers, the gentry who, unlike us, get a vote. Because his party opposed free trade with other nations—whereby Britain is at liberty to choose the lowest possible price for commodities from all over the world—people fully expected the cost of their food to rise.

The other thing that happened came a day or two later, by which point my ribs were healing, my wrist was on the mend, and Julius's nightmares had abated somewhat. It was a Wednesday evening. Julius and Bertha were sitting at the table, working on money together, when there came a tentative knock at the door.

'You gunna answer that, Octopus, or you just gunna sit there?' shouted Bertha.

I got up from my seat by the stove and went and opened the door. It was a new moon, so it was difficult to see who it was out on the landing. As the figure stepped forward into the light, I suddenly recognized Florrie, the girl who'd been minding Bertha's flower stall for him all this time. Though her shawl was pulled tightly round her shoulders, she still appeared to be shivering. Before I could open my mouth to call Bertha, Florrie placed her fingers across my lips to stop me.

'Bertha says the first assignation is free,' she whispered huskily, anchoring her body to mine, 'and nor will the second one cost ya. But even for you, the great Octopus, *there ain't no third unless it's a wedding!*'

AUTHOR'S NOTE

This novel was inspired by characters from Wilkie
Collins's *The Moonstone*, in particular the irrepressible
Octavius Guy—better known as Gooseberry. It was
originally published in weekly instalments throughout
the summer of 2014 on my author blog at Goodreads,
just as Collins's novel was first serialized in Charles
Dickens's magazine *All the Year Round* almost a hundred
and fifty years ago.

As I wrote "on the fly", so to speak—producing
one chapter per week without even the benefit of a
predetermined plot—I spent the month leading up to
the start of the project doing four essential things:
finding a suitable back story for Octavius; studying
the speech patterns of the characters I inherited from
Collins; creating some sustainable characters of my
own; and boning up on as much of the history of the
period as I could.

Most of what I've written has a basis in solid,
historical fact. For instance, much of Gooseberry's and
Johnny Knight's back story (concerning their career
path from mudlark to Ragged School student to thief)
is taken from the account of mudlarks in Henry
Mayhew's seminal work *London Labour and the London
Poor* of 1861.

But there are times when I took liberties with
history, and I would like the chance to set the record
straight. To the best of my knowledge, the Thames

Tunnel was never a venue of nightly debauchery. The idea suggested itself to me when I came across a contemporary review of the tunnel by a Frenchman, François Wey, who, in 1853, wrote, "*These booths ought certainly to be closed by the Government, both for the sake of hygiene and morality, as it is patent that trade here is only a thin cloak for prostitution*". It's almost certain that this was sour grapes on Wey's part, typical of the petty rivalry—on *both* sides—between France and Britain.

In real life, Duleep Singh's eyes bore no scars whatsoever. On the contrary, Queen Victoria, who later served as godmother to several of his children, once remarked of the young man, "*Those eyes and those teeth are too beautiful*". Equally, he was never the subject of a plot—at least, not in the sense of the one described here. The machinations of the East India Company to separate him from his mother and banish him to England are quite another matter, however. That part of the story is true. Nor am I aware of Dr Login ever running an asylum, in Twickenham or elsewhere. Cole Park Grange is a figment of my imagination, as is Sir Humphrey Mallard, as is the pub, the Jolly Boatman.

The Kohinoor diamond, presented to Queen Victoria by the East India Company after they fought and won the Second Anglo-Sikh War, went on display to the public in The Great Exhibition of 1851. The reaction was less than enthusiastic, however, for although the stone was at that point the largest diamond in the world, it "didn't catch the light," as Sergeant Cuff explains in chapter fifteen. A contemporary report in *The Times* puts it this way:

"*For some hours yesterday there were never less than a*

couple of hundred persons waiting their turn of admission, and yet, after all, the diamond does not satisfy. Either from the imperfect cutting or the difficulty of placing the lights advantageously, or the immovability of the stone itself, which should be made to revolve on its axis, few catch any of the brilliant rays it reflects when viewed at a particular angle."

So plans were made to have the diamond re-cut. Prince Albert took charge of the project, and the work was started in 1852…but not in January, as I suggest in the book. Rather, the work began in early July.

Finally, I thought I might share with you some details about the cover image, which I adore. It's by the Scottish-born Victorian photographer John Thomson, and it's entitled "The Cheap Fish of St. Giles's". The young man at the centre of the photo is Joseph Carney, who owns this barrow—based in a street market in London's Seven Dials district, near Covent Garden—from which he sells his fish. The young man at his side is a German friend of his, whose regular occupation is the hand-rolling of cigars.

On the day this photo was taken, Carney had snapped up a barrel of five hundred herrings at Billingsgate, the wholesale fish market, so his friend was roped in to help him gut and scale the fish. When I first saw this photo, I immediately pictured the boy with the ewer, who has his back to us, as Julius. Only later did I find out that, despite his height, he is in fact seventeen years old, and has already made one return voyage to South Africa by working as part of a ship's crew. If you look closely, the second face from the left belongs to an orphan named Ugly. Ugly manages to scrape a living by going from stall to stall, offering to do odd jobs and run errands. The second face from the right belongs to an older gent in a silk hat. He owns two properties in the neighbourhood and disapproves of the market, fearing that it lowers the tone of the area. This photograph was first published in *Street Life In London*, a collaboration between the photographer John Thomson and the writer Adolphe Smith. A free PDF download of the book is available from the London School of Economics' Digital Library: http://digital.library.lse.ac.uk/collections/streetlifeinlondon

Michael Gallagher, 2014.

And there's more...

Receipts Both Ancient and Modern

(Arranged in ascending order of complexity)

Property of
Octavius Guy

and his brother
Julius

Stove-baked Potatoes

Ingredients:
One goodly-sized potato per person

Method:
Wash the potatoes well to remove any dirt. Prick all over with a fork and bake on a trivet over the dying embers of your stove until cooked through.

[*Editor's note: A far superior result will be achieved thus: Wash the potatoes well and dry them thoroughly. Prick all over with a fork, rub the surface first with oil and then with coarsely ground sea salt. Bake on an open shelf (no tray required, but place a drip tray on a shelf below) for 1½ hours in a moderately hot oven, gas mark 5; 190°C (375°F); lower for a fan-assisted oven. Split and serve with lashings of butter and a sprinkling of ground black pepper, or a dollop of sour cream and chives. Delicious! Suitable for vegetarians.*]

Spiced Carrot Soup

Ingredients:
1 lb. carrots
1 onion
1 clove of garlic
1½ oz. butter
3 teaspoons ground coriander
a pinch of cayenne pepper
2 teaspoons flour
1¼ pints of good, well seasoned vegetable stock
a squeeze of lemon juice
chopped coriander to taste, plus whole leaves for garnish
¾ cup of milk
a square of greaseproof paper, a little larger than the diameter of the saucepan

Method:
Peel carrots, onions, and garlic, and chop roughly. Melt the butter in a saucepan, add the vegetables and stir to coat. Cook gently for 2 minutes, turn down the heat, and press the greaseproof paper over the vegetables to cover, so that very little steam escapes and the vegetables sweat gently for a further 20 minutes.

Remove the paper, stir in the ground coriander and cayenne pepper, and then the flour, then let this cook for 2 minutes or so. Add the vegetable stock, stirring well, and bring to the boil. Simmer for half an hour.

Allow to cool a little, strain the stock into a bowl,

then press the vegetables through a fine sieve with the back of a wooden spoon. Combine the puree and the stock.*

Add a squeeze of lemon juice and some finely chopped coriander to taste. Stir, then add the milk. Transfer the soup back into the saucepan, and gently bring it back to a simmer, stirring all the while. Serve garnished with whole coriander leaves.

[*Editor's note: it's much easier to use a blender at this point. Suitable for vegetarians.]

Coconut Macaroons

Ingredients:
2 egg whites
6 oz. castor sugar
3 oz. desiccated coconut
½ teaspoon almond essence
rice-wafer paper
[*Editor's note: rice-wafer paper is the traditional base, but if unavailable, sprinkle a light dusting of ground almonds (or ground rice, or, at a pinch, even a little corn flour) on some non-stick baking parchment and use this instead.*]

Method:
Whisk egg whites till frothy. Continue whisking, adding the sugar bit by bit till the mixture is stiff, then beat in the essence. Fold in the coconut. Line baking trays with rice-wafer paper, then carefully arrange spoonfuls of the mixture on top, leaving a 2" gap between each biscuit. Bake for 25 minutes in a moderate oven until the macaroons are lightly browned and firm to the touch. Cut away the excess wafer when cold.

[*Editor's note: gas mark 3; 160°C (325°F); lower for a fan-assisted oven. For traditional macaroons, substitute an equal quantity of ground almonds for the coconut, and place a split almond on top of each biscuit before baking. Suitable for vegetarians.*]

Bakewell Tart

Except for the bashing of the almonds, an extremely
light hand is required throughout.

For the pastry:
5¼ oz. flour
2½ oz. castor sugar
2½ oz. very cold butter
2 egg yolks

Method:
Sift the flour and sugar together. Cut the chilled
butter into small cubes and add it to the flour. Using
only the tips of your fingers, gently work the butter
into the flour until the texture resembles that of
breadcrumbs. Beat the egg yolks with a fork, add
them to the paste, then use a table knife to work them
in. Give the pastry a gentle knead, cover, and set aside
to chill for an hour.

[*Editor's note: the left-over egg whites can be used to make
Macaroons—see previous recipe.*]

For the filling:
4½ oz. whole almonds, skin on
4¼ oz. castor sugar
2 oz. butter
3 eggs
1-2 drops vanilla extract
raspberry jam

Method:

Grind the almonds well. Place in a mixing bowl with the sugar, then bash the two together to release the almonds' natural oils. Cream in the softened butter. Add one of the eggs, together with the vanilla extract, and beat quite vigorously until the mixture turns pale and thick. Separate the remaining eggs, then beat in the yolks one at a time. Now, using a clean bowl and a whisk, *gently* beat the whites until they form stiff peaks. Fold a spoonful of the beaten whites into the almond batter to loosen it, then *gently* fold the batter into the whites, using a tablespoon with a cutting and lifting motion to retain as much of the trapped air as possible.

Roll out the pastry and line a greased 9" round flan tin. Spread raspberry jam around the base and top with the batter. Level carefully with a palette knife. Bake for 45 minutes in a moderately hot oven. Allow to cool completely before slicing.

[*Editor's note: gas mark 5; 190°C (375°F); lower for a fan-assisted oven. Suitable for vegetarians.*]

Kedgeree

Ingredients:
1 cup rice
2 eggs, simmered very gently for 10 minutes until hard boiled
8 oz. smoked cod *or* smoked haddock
½ cup peas
2 oz. butter
1 onion
1 clove of garlic, crushed
1 teaspoon each of ground cumin and coriander
½ teaspoon of turmeric
¼ teaspoon of a good garam masala
parsley or coriander [cilantro] leaves to garnish
wedges of lemon to serve

Method:
If possible, cook the rice and the eggs the day before, and chill overnight. Poach the fish gently in a little water or milk until it separates easily into flakes. Cook the peas. Peel and chop the eggs. Finely chop the onion.

Melt the butter in a large frying pan. Add the onion and cook gently for 12 - 15 minutes, stirring occasionally, until softened. Add the garlic and the cumin, coriander, and turmeric, and cook for a further 2 minutes. Then add the rice, stirring occasionally, until thoroughly heated through. Gently stir in the peas, then the flaked smoked fish. Arrange on a warm serving platter, sprinkle over the garam masala, followed by the chopped eggs, and then parsley or coriander [cilantro]. Serve with wedges of lemon. Enough for two hungry people, or three or four with accompanying side dishes.

Gooseberry Chutney

Ingredients:
3 lb. gooseberries
4 oz. onions
1 lb. cooking apples, peeled and cored
12 oz. stoned dates
8 oz. brown sugar
1 teaspoon salt
a pinch or two of ground cayenne pepper
1 pint malt vinegar
a piece of root ginger, the size of your thumb
1 teaspoon mustard seeds

Method:
Top and tail the gooseberries. Chop the onion moderately fine. Roughly chop the apples and dates. Peel the ginger, then bash it with the side of a cleaver. Tie up the ginger and mustard seeds in a square of clean muslin, then place all the ingredients in a saucepan, the larger the better. Bring to the boil and simmer in the open pan for 1 hour, or until the mixture has thickened up nicely. Remove the muslin spice bag, and pour the hot mixture into equally hot, sterilized jars, then seal. Allow the chutney to mature for at least six weeks before opening. Enjoy with a wedge of good cheddar cheese or a pork pie, or serve with cold roasted meats. Makes approximately 3-4 lbs.

[*Editor's note: Suitable for vegetarians.*]

And even more…

OCTOPUS
Octavius Guy & The Case of the Throttled Tragedienne (#2)

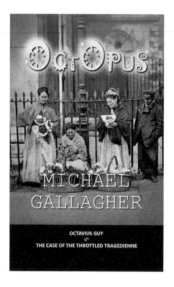

When the leading actress dies in mysterious circumstances on stage during a performance of The Duchess of Malfi at the Sadler's Wells Theatre, Gooseberry feels duty-bound to investigate. It is, after all, a great deal more exciting than the last case he was assigned to: the tracking down of a rich old lady's errant cat!

Join Octavius (AKA Gooseberry, AKA Octopus) and his ragtag bunch of friends on their second adventure, a revenge tragedy (of sorts) in (roughly—*very* roughly) three acts.

Published by Seventh Rainbow Publishing, London Available now at Amazon.com and other online stores.

Fancy a sneak peek? Read on...

THE PROLOGUE

London. Thursday, July 1st, 1852; 9.30 pm.

THE APRON STAGE AT Sadler's Wells is a large one; it extends well beyond the theatre's proscenium arch, which marks the traditional boundary to any normal stage. Our private box was situated directly above it, which meant we got a bird's-eye view of the proceedings.

I've seen plays before—well, maybe not *plays* exactly, but I've seen *a play*. Ned, the one-time leader of London's criminal underworld, took me to see it just before he made me his deuce…his second-in-command, that's to say. It was called "*Macbeth*", and for nigh on three hours I sat transfixed. The blood! The gore! All a young boy could wish for! Afterwards he asked me what I thought the moral of the story was. I considered replying, 'Go trafficking with witches at your peril,' which seemed like a perfectly appropriate moral to me, but I found myself saying, 'You shouldn't betray someone's trust, the way that Macbeth betrayed Duncan's.' He seemed to appreciate this answer, for he smiled and slapped me on the back. Of course, this was a lifetime ago—well, half of my lifetime, at least—before I was reformed of my felonious ways and began taking my responsibilities more seriously.

If you find it hard to believe that a criminal overlord would make a seven-year-old boy his deuce, let me tell you there are reasons, good reasons, which will no doubt become obvious to you, astute reader, long before you and I finish this tale.

The play I was currently enjoying, *The Duchess of Malfi*, concerned itself with the greed and corruption that can fester even in the highest-born families. Oh, the poor duchess! She had no chance of happiness, not with brothers like hers! Her despicable siblings distrusted her so, they planted a spy in her household. Their man, a fellow named Bosola, was for ever wrestling with his conscience, for he could see that the duchess was pure at heart, whereas his spy masters were naught but evil.

I was beginning to despair of any bloodthirstiness, however, for so far there had not been a single death. Mercifully, with the arrival of act four—and a new set of orders for the troubled Mr Bosola—this oversight was about to be addressed.

First the spy drove the duchess to despair by showing her the bodies of her slaughtered offspring (waxworks, one and all—not that she was aware of the fact—but my point is, *as waxworks*, they can hardly be included in the final body count, now can they?). Ah, but I digress!

Next he tried to taunt her by filling her house with madmen. That didn't go too well for him, for by now she was indifferent to their company.

It forced him to put his final humiliation for her into play. A tingle—a thrill—ran down my spine as he ushered his band of assassins on stage. They were dressed as monks, and with their cowls drawn over their heads it was impossible to see anything of their faces. How exquisitely creepy they looked!

'Pull, and pull strongly,' the duchess cried out, as they each strung a cord round her neck.

Oh, but she was a feisty one! Refusing to utter so much as a whimper, she writhed and convulsed in heart-rending silence before crumpling in a heap on the floor. Any caterwauling was left up to the big, brawny chambermaid—who was next for the chop— as the thugs dragged her screaming from the stage. I had to sit on my hands to stop myself clapping! And, yes, even *I* know you clap at the end of an act and not at some point in the middle—well, I do now, having clapped at a seemingly inappropriate moment during *Macbeth*.

The leading actress, Miss Prynn—or Bella, as I'd already begun to think of her again, for it turned out that I'd known her in the past—had given us a sterling performance as the throttled duchess. Even now she lay face-up and motionless on the stage some fifteen feet below me. So perfect was the effect, in fact, that, in the narrow beam of limelight that fell across her throat, I could have sworn I saw signs of actual bruising. I was only sorry that our host, Mr Willoughby, had had to miss all the fun, having withdrawn from the box some time earlier to answer a call of nature.

When one of the brothers who'd come to gloat

over her corpse eventually made his exit, Bosola stood surveying the duchess's body, then suddenly gave a start.

'She stirs, here's life!' he marvelled, hurrying to her side. 'Return, fair soul, from darkness and lead mine out of this sensible hell.'

The actor knelt down and, grasping Bella's hand, raked her fingers along his smooth, jutting jaw.

'She's warm, she breathes,' he murmured. 'Upon thy pale lips I will melt my heart, to store them with fresh colour.'

He leaned forward and kissed her. Everybody in the theatre leaned forward too.

'Her eye opes…'

He was staring down at her face, as were we, so we could see just as he could that her eyelids hadn't budged.

'Her *eye* opes…'

This time he said it louder, emphasizing the words, but still to no effect as far as I could see. Both Bella's eyes remained stubbornly closed.

'HER EYE OPES…'

He was almost shouting the line now, and I could hear the panic in his voice.

'You said that twice already!' came a heckler from the balcony. A number of people burst out laughing.

Mr Jacobs—the actor playing Bosola—rose to his feet and approached the front of the stage. White-faced and trembling, he addressed the audience directly: 'Ladies and gentlemen, I beg your forgiveness. Miss Prynn appears to have been taken ill.'

A low, rumbling mutter started somewhere in the dress circle, then spread rapidly to other sections of the building.

'Ladies and gentlemen, please,' Mr Jacobs appealed over the din, 'is there a doctor in the house?'

Mr Bone, a man whose acquaintance we'd only just made whilst on our way to the theatre, sprang up from his chair beside me. He was obviously intending to help, but was unsure quite how to proceed. All of a sudden he spied a figure racing down the aisle of the stalls. 'Look,' he said, pointing.

As we watched, the fellow hopped the barrier into the orchestra pit, then hauled himself on to the stage. He knelt beside Bella and, after loosening her ruff, he felt for a pulse in her wrist. The mumblings in the auditorium faded to a whisper.

The man removed his hat and bent over Bella, obscuring our view of her face.

'The procedure he's attempting is known as mouth-to-mouth resuscitation,' Mr Bone informed us tensely.

Since he claimed to have some medical training, I could only assume he knew what he was talking about. I could see the rise and fall of Bella's chest with every breath the man delivered, but apart from this she remained unnaturally still. After what seemed like an age, he stopped what he was doing and leaned back on his haunches.

'What's going on here?' asked Mr Willoughby, as he made his way back to his seat. 'Did I miss summat while I was away?'

His return to the box was met with a '*Shush!*'

Frowning at this unexpected reception—for he'd been the one to fork out for this evening's enter-tainment—he sat himself down with as much dignity as he could muster and peered over the balustrade with the rest of us.

'Miss Prynn's been taken poorly,' my employer whispered in his ear. 'That's the doctor with her now.'

'I fear one of the executioners may have got a little over-zealous with his cord,' muttered his partner-in-the-making, the flashily-dressed Mr Peacock.

Mr Willoughby shot him a look. 'Then why's the doctor doing nowt? Why don't he try to bring her round?'

'He *has* tried to revive her,' explained Mr Bone, with a touch of exasperation in his voice. 'He's just sent backstage for a hand mirror.'

'A hand mirror? What the heck for? That lass is in no state to be fussing with make-up!'

'He'll want to check for her breath on the glass, sir. It's exactly what I would do in his position. Look, someone is bringing one now.'

An actress, who'd had a very minor role in the play, entered from the wings, carrying a mirror. She passed it to the doctor, who held it first to Bella's mouth and then up to her nose.

'"*O fly your fate. Thou art a dead thing. Never see her more,*"' intoned Mr Bone, and, though he was murmuring these phrases under his breath, in the silence that had fallen in the auditorium we all heard every word.

'What's he on about?' demanded Mr Willoughby.

Mr Bone looked at him and blinked. 'They're lines from later in the play, sir, that the duchess speaks from her grave. It seemed an appropriate tribute to the late Miss Prynn.'

'*The late*—?'

'Miss Isabella Prynn. She is dead, sir. She is dead.'

My former friend, with whom I'd just been reunited, dead? How had a day that had started out so promisingly come to such a dreadful pass?

Five-star praise for the series
SEND FOR OCTAVIUS GUY

"Sometimes you see a book and just know you're going to love it...An absolute treat for fans of Collins' novel [The Moonstone] and a successful novel in its own right."
—Emma Hamilton, buriedunderbooks.co.uk, LibraryThing Early Reviewer
★ ★ ★ ★ ★

"Here is a sensational historical fiction who-dunnit that gives nothing away until the very end. To me, it reads like an old time radio show. It leaves you breathless."
—Connie A., LibraryThing Early Reviewer
★ ★ ★ ★ ★

"This is an absolute gem of a series and quite the most enjoyable set of books I have read in a very long time."
—Anita Dow, Goodreads Reviewer
★ ★ ★ ★ ★

"Thank you so much for writing these books, and for bringing these characters to life. I have a feeling they'll always be lurking around in my head. Excellent, excellent, excellent!"
—Laura Brook, LibraryThing Early Reviewer
★ ★ ★ ★ ★

"I was hooked from the start and spent as much time trying to guess the outcome as I did laughing out loud. I thoroughly enjoyed this novel and can't wait to read another of Mr. Gallagher's mysteries. Forget Sherlock Holmes, send for Octavius Guy!"
—Brittney L. Divine, author, Smashwords Reviewer
★ ★ ★ ★ ★

"My favorite Victorian boy investigator sets off to solve a new mystery…Words cannot describe just how much I enjoy Octavius."
—Bethany Swafford (TheQuietReader), Goodreads Reviewer
★★★★★

"Michael Gallagher is a marvellous writer and storyteller. Witty, warm, full of wonderful descriptions, dialogue and characters. Doesn't sound like a murder mystery? It certainly is."
—Alasdair Muckersie, Goodreads Reviewer
★★★★★

"A scholarly murder mystery without being staid…a masterpiece of misdirection and layers of creative storytelling. Trust me. Buy the books!"
—Laura Dogsmom (Laura in Wisconsin), Goodreads Reviewer
★★★★★

"Did I solve the puzzle - no, but I enjoyed every minute of Octopus's investigations."
—LizzieKillin (Liz Stevens), LibraryThing Early Reviewer
★★★★★

"When you read a book by Michael Gallagher be prepared for a total immersion—every bit of scene setting, speech, character and historical detail is perfect."
—Chris Keen LibraryThing Early Reviewer
★★★★★

"Pour some tea or a wee dram, put your feet up, and enjoy cover to cover."
—Gladread, LibraryThing Early Reviewer
★★★★★

ABOUT THE AUTHOR

Author Photo by Elaine Jeffs

Michael Gallagher is the author of two series of novels set in Victorian times. *Send for Octavius Guy* chronicles the attempts of fourteen-year-old Gooseberry—reformed master pickpocket—to become a detective, aided and abetted by his ragtag bunch of friends. *The Involuntary Medium* follows the fortunes of young Lizzie Blaylock, a girl who can materialize the spirits of the dead, as she strives to come to terms with her unique gift.

For twenty-five years Michael taught adults with learning disabilities at Bede, a London-based charity that works with the local community. He now writes full time.

Find him online:
on Twitter @seventh7rainbow
at his website michaelgallagherwrites.com
and on Facebook and Goodreads.

Follow Octavius Guy @sendforOctavius.